DETERMINED

Lipstick and Lead Book 5

BY SYLVIA MCDANIEL

Books by Sylvia McDaniel

Contemporary Romance

Standalones
The Reluctant Santa
My Sister's Boyfriend
The Wanted Bride
The Relationship Coach
Her Christmas Lie
Secrets, Lies, and Online Dating
Paying for the Past
Cupid's Revenge

Anthologies
Kisses, Laughter & Love
Christmas with you

Collaborative Series

Magic, New Mexico
Touch of Decadence

Western Historicals

Standalones
A Hero's Heart
A Scarlet Bride
Second Chance Cowboy

The Cuvier Women
Wronged
Betrayed
Beguiled

Lipstick and Lead
Desperate
Deadly
Dangerous
Daring
Determined
Deceived

Scandalous Suffragettes
Abigail
Bella
Callie
Faith

The Burnett Brides
The Rancher Takes a Bride
The Outlaw Takes a Bride
The Marshal Takes a Bride
The Christmas Bride

Anthologies
Wild Western Women
Courting the West
Wild Western Women Ride Again

Collaborative Series

The Surprise Brides
Ethan

American Mail Order Brides
Katie

Determined
Published by Virtual Bookseller

Cover Design by Lyndsey Lewellen
https://lyndseylewellen.wordpress.com/

Edited by Andrea Dickinson
http://www.qualitybookservices.com/

Formatted by Laurelle Procter
laurelleprocter@gmail.com

Short Description: Hannah Williams is looking for revenge against the man who sold her into prostitution. Preacher Jackson Colster is determined to stop her.

ISBN: 978-1-942608-55-4 (paperback)
ISBN: 978-1-942608-04-2 (e-book)

{Historical Western Romance – Fiction}

www.SylviaMcDaniel.com

Synopsis

Hannah Williams' first goal after becoming a bounty hunter is to return to Hide Town, Texas to seek revenge on the man who sold her into prostitution. While searching for her stepfather, she stumbles across a man brutally beaten and takes him to her hideout. There, she is horrified to discover she has rescued the very man who turned his back on her during her blackest moment.

Preacher Jackson Colster never imagined the girl he refused to help would one day return to town and save his life. Now he must save Hannah from her destructive path of retribution while resisting the lure of her determined spirit. Or in mending her damaged past, will she help him confront his own haunting nightmares?

Can Hannah and Jackson heal their wounds, silence the past, and let love guide their future?

Table of Contents

Chapter One

Hannah Williams knew life was hard. This past year had shown her she could never let her guard down, or she'd suffer the consequences. That very guard was firmly in place as she watched a man beaten while she hid in the bushes on the outskirts of Hide Town, Texas.

In this town, the bad guys were in control, and she'd returned to get revenge on the people who'd changed her life forever—to reclaim her good name and kill the man responsible for her misfortune and the woman who'd helped him.

From the shadows, she watched the madam's three goons beat the man who hung limply between them, no longer fighting. His face was bloodied, his eyes already swelling shut, his lip cracked and bleeding.

Oh, how she wanted to scurry away, leave him and the goons, and mind her own business. But what if Ruby hadn't rescued her? What if six months ago she'd ridden away, leaving Hannah behind?

"Enough," one of the men said. "I think he's damn near dead."

"Let's go," the ringleader said. "It's getting close to dark, and I've got things to do besides beat a stupid man."

"What about the girl?"

Hannah sank back deeper into the shadows. What girl were they talking about? While she'd returned to town seeking retribution, she wasn't ready to show herself just yet.

"She's not here. He must have gotten her out of town."

"Damn, she was a pretty one. I was looking forward to getting me a piece of that young'un."

Alarm spiraled through Hannah, yet she wasn't afraid. Her resolve strengthened, and she reached down and felt the gun at her side. Lovingly, she touched the revolver, knowing she didn't fear using it on any man who would harm her.

"If you think she's so gorgeous, you chase her into a town where the sheriff doesn't look the other way. You'll be looking down her father's rifle in no time with a village full of people ready to string you up for hurting one of their own."

Another young girl must have been captured, and they'd tried to force her into prostitution.

Dropping the man's arms, they let him fall to the ground. "Let's leave him for the coyotes."

One of the men gave the senseless man a swift kick in the ribs. The body on the ground moved but didn't make a sound. She wondered if he was dead.

The outlaws climbed on their horses. Hannah watched as they spurred them and rode off in the semi-darkness. Now what did she do?

Creeping out of the shadows, she hurried to the man on the ground and rolled him over. He groaned, letting her know he lived. There was little time in case the goons returned. The beaten man had one chance to get on her horse, or she was leaving him behind.

She shook him. Slowly, he opened his swollen eyelids and tried to gaze at her.

"Do you want to live?" she asked, knowing they needed to get out of here before the outlaws circled back to finish the job they'd started and found them both.

He groaned.

"If you want to live, you've got to help me get you on my horse. I can't do this alone."

There was no way she could get him in the saddle without his help, and there was no way he could walk. And there was no way she was staying here on the prairie tonight without a fire.

"Leave me. Let me die," he groaned. "I'll be in a better place."

Shaking her head, she started to walk away and then went back, unable to do as he requested. "Better hope the coyotes don't find you before you die. Because there are a lot of those critters around here, and they're hungry. They like to play with their food for a while before they rip into the carcass. You'll taste pretty yummy to them."

"All right, you made your point."

She watched as the man crawled to his knees, shaking his head. Rushing to his side, she helped him to his feet. Placing her arms beneath his armpits, she supported him as he hobbled to her horse. "What did you do that angered the madam's goons?"

"You're in danger," he managed to mumble between swollen lips. "Leave me."

"I live with danger," she spat out. She had only one goal left worth living for. After that, she didn't care what happened to her. But she wasn't dying until her revenge was complete. If it took her fighting from the pit of hell, she'd settle the score for losing her innocence and the killing of her mother.

Helping him crawl up on her horse, she climbed up behind him. He leaned forward, hugging the animal's neck, barely able to ride, and she feared he would fall before they could reach the abandoned shack she'd claimed as her own.

"What's your name?" she asked.

"Jackson Colster," he muttered through swollen lips.

At the name, anger rushed through her like a strong wind. This ugly man was the damn preacher who had turned his back on her when she'd tried to escape, the very man who her mother had gone to and told she feared her husband. His only response was to tell her that marriage was forever.

This preacher man? Hannah hadn't cared whether he

lived or died so why was she now helping him to live?

The urge to push him off her horse and leave him behind was strong, but Hannah was not going to be a hypocrite like the one she had riding on her horse. She'd give him shelter, doctor his wounds, and send him on his way.

While she prepared for the coming battle.

~

Jackson slipped in and out of consciousness as they rode through the darkness. He knew he was lucky to be alive, though at this second, he wished he would die. There wasn't a spot on his body that didn't throb, even his big toe felt like they'd taken a hammer to the digit. For a moment, he'd thought an angel had arrived to take him to heaven, but when she said she was leaving him for the coyotes, he knew he was still here on earth.

Someone had rescued him, and that didn't feel right.

The horse stopped, and the girl slipped over the side. "Come on, we're here."

He had no idea where *here* was, but at least his sore body wouldn't be bouncing on the back of a slow moving horse. Gingerly, he slid his leg over the side and let his torso slide down the animal. When his feet touched the ground, he would have fallen, except there were two small strong hands there steadying him.

"Where are we?"

"An abandoned shack," she said. "I'm sorry, but there are no fires and no lights."

"Why not?" he asked, not really caring, but wondering just the same.

"Don't need any unwanted company," she said, vague in her response.

There was no way he could survive another beating, so

he was fine hiding out.

They took a step toward the cabin, and he wanted to groan with the smallest movement, but he bit his lip to hold in his response.

"Just a little further, and then we'll get you settled for the night."

"Thank you," he said softly, knowing he owed this woman for saving his life.

"Don't thank me," she said, her voice tense in the darkness. "I didn't save you because I like you. I saved you because someone else rescued me. I'm just paying back the universe for sending someone who had the courage to get me out of that hellhole."

Like a bolt of lightning striking the ground in front of him, he recognized the young woman.

The whore who had begged him to liberate her from the madam. At the time, he'd been new to town and believed she'd willingly chosen her lifestyle. Now, he knew different. Now, he knew the ugly truth surrounding the way the madam acquired her new girls.

Hannah Williams was the girl he'd refused to help, the one he'd always regretted turning his back on. "Hannah, why did you return?"

"Only one reason, preacher man. Revenge. You're just lucky I'm not interested in killing you for your lack of compassion."

Preacher man came out sounding like an insult, a slur to his profession. She had every right to be angry with him, but right now he just couldn't feel any worse than he already did. And he'd stolen the last young girl from the madam.

"I didn't save you, but you rescued me."

"I damn sure did. Shows I have more compassion than you do."

He sighed. Being a man of God was never easy, and

Hannah had been one of his many failings. "I wish you hadn't come back."

"Why?"

"You should have ridden as far from this town as possible. I don't know if it's worth liberating." How do you save a town filled with the worst of humanity? Yet, he'd done what he could to help the innocent lives that were forced to live in this Sodom and Gomorrah.

"Who says I want to save the town?"

He turned to gaze at the young, beautiful woman. Hate seemed to ooze from her body and he couldn't blame her. "Why would you return?" he asked again.

"My destiny is to kill the people who harmed me. And I aim to do just that."

Killing would not bring her the restitution she craved. Maybe not today, but sometime in the future she would regret her vengeful actions. He knew from experience that taking another man's life haunted a person's spirit. Eventually the realization of what she'd done would eat away at her soul like a cancer.

~

The next morning Hannah watched Jackson sleeping on the small bed in the center of the cabin. He really needed a doctor, but she didn't know of one in town who wouldn't rush to the sheriff and tell him of Jackson's injuries. So instead, she would see if the stable boy would get her the supplies she needed to take care of Jackson's wounds herself. Unless he was close to dying, they were on their own.

And if he died…not a great loss in her opinion. One less negligent person in a town of fools.

He stirred in the bed, moaning. "Melissa."

Who's Melissa? Rising from the hard floor where she'd

spent the night, Hannah gazed over at him, and he opened his eyes. "Good morning."

Last night, Jackson had passed out the moment she got him in the bed. Then she'd removed his clothes and bathed his injuries.

She watched as he lifted the sheet and realized he was naked as the day he'd been brought into this world. "You took my clothes."

A smile flitted across her face at the memory. She'd seen the preacher naked and enjoyed the sight of his male body. "Yes, I did," she said, scooping some water for him.

He drank greedily from the dipper. "You saw me naked."

"Honey, you're not the first man I've seen naked. Last I checked, parts are all the same."

With a snort, he leaned back against the pillows. "But they're my parts and I don't let just anyone see them."

"Too bad," she said with a shrug. "They weren't all that bad."

A blush came over his cheeks, and she knew she'd gotten to him. *Good.* He deserved to be uncomfortable for as long as possible.

She moved around the cabin, putting the dipper back in the pail of water, before she found the hard tack biscuits she'd stored.

"You got away. Why did you come back?"

His memory from last night must be foggy because she was certain they'd discussed this on the ride to the lean-to. "Simple. Revenge."

Vindication was what had got her through the long days and nights of having sex with faceless men. Retribution was what she had for breakfast every morning, and payback was what fed her at supper. Soon, she would wreak havoc on the people who'd harmed her.

"Revenge is the devil's advocate," he said with a sigh.

"Yes, preacher man, it is, and I fully expect to go to hell, but I'll be following the people who ruined my life." For a moment, she missed the fun-loving girl she'd once been before her mother had died and her stepfather had sold her to the madam for a gambling debt he owed. He would be the first bastard she shot.

With a sigh, Jackson gazed at her, his brown eyes shining through the slits of his swollen lids. "I'm not a preacher man anymore. My congregation deserted me. God has deserted me, and my faith is shattered. I'm nothing."

She stared at him. While she could see the pain in his eyes and hear it in his voice, it was still hard to feel sympathy. She'd asked for his help, and he'd told her to return to the bordello where she belonged. "You're a man of God, or you wouldn't have become a preacher."

Turning his head, he glanced out the window. "I think I made a mistake. I should never have taken up the ministry."

If he was looking for sympathy, he wasn't getting it from her. Her well had run dry a long time ago. She wasn't certain what had pushed him to think he wasn't a good minister, and frankly, she didn't care.

Standing, she gazed at him. This morning the bruises were clearly visible, and his face was starting to turn black and blue. His lips were cracked, and she could tell it cost him a lot just to talk.

"Oh, you've made some mistakes. We all have. Welcome to the land of sinners." For months, she'd hated this man. She'd wasted one of her opportunities to leave town on seeking his help, and he'd turned her away.

"I'm sorry, Hannah. I let you down."

Oh no, he was not getting off this easy. In her darkest hour, he'd rebuffed her. Just saying *I'm sorry* was not going to make the shame go away.

"No, you weren't there for me. But a girl I'd never seen

before, she not only saved my life, she gave me purpose. Unlike you, she's someone I can depend on. I'm forever in Ruby McKenzie's debt."

"And now I'm in your debt."

She didn't want him in arrears to her. It felt wrong, yet part of her couldn't help but laugh at the way life had him beholden to her.

Taking another hardtack biscuit out, she handed it to him. "Eat up. This is breakfast, lunch, and dinner."

He shook his head. "I'm not hungry."

"Eat it anyway," she said coldly. "The sooner you get well, the sooner we go our separate ways."

She sank down on the bed and ate her biscuit. The logical part of her mind said she needed to feel compassion for this broken man, but the girl who had lost everything felt no remorse. He'd turned his back on her, and she'd spent another month in that hellhole of a brothel servicing men.

A shudder rippled through her, almost gagging her at the ugliness in her past. That was behind her; she'd die before she went back into that whorehouse. Now she had a gun, she knew how to use it, and she wouldn't think twice about killing anyone who tried to force her into that den of inequity. In fact, she almost relished the thought of the madam and her goons coming for her.

They'd be dead men walking.

"How do you plan on getting revenge?" he asked. "Don't you think they'll be waiting for you?"

Right now, she had no set plan, except to find her stepfather. Once she found and killed him, she would come back for the madam. Then she would release the girls from their servitude.

Sure, some of the women had chosen that lifestyle, but others had not, and those women, Hannah wanted to help escape. Somewhere, they could begin anew.

Funny, she didn't see her life past this moment in time. This was her destiny. Maybe even her death.

"No. Who would suspect sweet little Hannah Williams would return and bring about vengeance?" she said bitterly. "I'm going to rescue the girls, give them their freedom, and put an end to Madam Hutchins' reign of terror on this town."

"What about the sheriff? How are you going to stop him?"

She smiled. "The same way I plan on stopping the madam. One bullet at a time."

His face grimaced in pain, and she realized he was hurting. "Do you want another sip of water?"

"No," he said, shifting in the bed. "I hurt all over. A good dose of whiskey would ease the pain."

"Sorry, I don't drink," she said, remembering how her mother would not allow alcohol in their home. How she'd taught her to be a lady. A God-fearing woman who attended church each Sunday and read her Bible each night.

"They busted you up pretty bad," she said. "It's a wonder you're not dead."

"Hannah, I know you want to kill the people who hurt you. But take it from me, killing someone doesn't make you feel good. In the end, you'll regret taking their life, even though they deserved to die."

"How do you know, preacher man?"

He sighed, his big brown eyes glazed with pain. "Thou shall not kill, but I did."

Shock trickled down her spine, leaving her dazed and confused. The *supposed* man of God had killed someone. It seemed they both had secrets.

Chapter Two

Mrs. Emily Hutchins, owner of the local saloon and the madam of its upstairs brothel, knew a sucker when she saw one. And Elliott Potter was about as dumb as a rock, but also easy for her to manipulate. She used him like a fiddler used a bow to get what she needed.

"It's not my fault the preacher stole the girl. Why am I being blamed for something you didn't have under control?" Elliott asked.

She frowned at him, not appreciating his response. "We're in this business together. We lost a new recruit. We should replace her. You're my main guy in getting new girls for the house. I want you to find me another one. Someone who is pretty and shy. Someone I can intimidate to follow the rules and learn her place."

They were working together only as long as she needed him or found someone else to bring her new recruits. Once she was done with Elliott, she'd use the sheriff to take care of him, just like she did anyone who gave her trouble in town. In fact, right about now, Jackson Colster was receiving a fine dose of Hide Town discipline. The preacher was probably meeting his maker because he'd interfered with the profitability of her brothel. Interfere and die.

"If we're working together, why do I feel like I'm taking all the risks?"

"You're not taking all the risks. I live in peril all the time. It comes with owning a brothel."

He frowned, and she knew she needed to curb this rebellion in a hurry. "Elliott, your stepdaughter cost me money. I could make you repay me what I gave you for her. Is that what you want?"

She watched as he carefully considered her words, his brows drawn together on his rugged face. Years ago, he must have been quite the looker, but hard living had caused lines around his eyes, and the skin around his jaw was beginning to sag. Not a man she'd let in her bed.

"No, let's keep things the same. I'll get busy trying to locate us another girl. But this time, you have to make certain she doesn't get away. This is two that have gotten away from you."

The man was right, but she would never admit to him that it was her fault her posse had become lax. She'd already had a talk with Hank about making certain no one else escaped the brothel. She didn't need her girls thinking there was a chance all of them could break out from the bordello. No one could leave, until she thought they were no longer an asset to her business.

"When do you plan on going?"

With a frown, he shook his head. "I'll ride out at daylight and travel over to Dyersville to see if there's any girl there we could use. This last girl I picked off north of Fort Worth. I don't want to hit the same area twice. Too big a chance of getting caught."

She smiled and patted him on the arm, rewarding him for coming around to her way of thinking. "I'm depending on you to find a beautiful, young girl that will fit in nicely with my other girls. You do such a good job."

Not really, but she was trying to make him more enthusiastic about finding the girls she needed. Sure, he didn't like taking an innocent girl from her family, but Emily liked young women in her brothel. And Elliott was good at locating what they needed. He was now her official girl-napper, and she planned on using him for quite some time.

"I'll be back as soon as possible," he said.

"Be careful. I don't want to lose my best man."

He smiled. "Maybe we could have dinner sometime."

That would never happen, but he didn't need to know that just yet. "Of course, you come back, and we'll talk about it." She smiled at him, giving the man her best come-and-get-it look, knowing it was a false promise.

Men were so gullible. Years ago, she'd learned they were so easily manipulated to do her will.

~

Hannah snuck into town, knowing she was taking a huge risk, but needing supplies. With the two of them sharing food, she was quickly running out of everything. The little shack had a well, so they were good with water, but she needed food and some medical supplies for Jackson. She'd made a list, and she hoped she could convince the stable boy to help her. He'd been a friend years ago.

Peering around the corner of the barn, she saw her stepfather talking to the boy she'd gone to school with. Tim still looked like a young boy, only she knew he was eighteen, just like herself. Those days seemed like a thousand years ago, and her chest tightened with pain at the memory of those happy days—her father lifting her on his shoulders, her mother's smiling face.

Then her death.

To this day, Hannah wondered if Elliott had killed her. He'd said he'd found her lying at the bottom of the brothel stairs, but why would her mother be in the saloon? Up in the brothel?

Unless she'd been looking for him.

And where were the witnesses? The parlor only sat empty early in the morning when the whores had yet to rise and face another day.

Tim, the stable boy, nodded to him. "Will do, sir."

Hannah had to resist the urge to pull out her six-shooter and blast her stepfather away. She wanted to rush into the barn and kill the bastard for what he'd done, but she knew the time wasn't right. The sheriff would love nothing better than to hang her for murder. The preacher was in no condition to ride, and they'd find him in the shanty.

No, she had to do this the right way at the right time.

Time was on her side. She'd soon get her day, and her stepfather would pay for the death of her mother and for selling Hannah into prostitution.

She waited for him to walk out of the barn and down the street. Taking a deep breath, she controlled the shaking of her hands and legs. He had no idea how close to dying he'd just come.

Scampering into the barn, she saw the young man. "Tim."

He looked up, his eyes widening. "What are you doing here? I thought you left town."

"I did. But I'm back."

"Are you crazy?"

She smiled. Before she'd always thought he was a little sweet on her, but that was before she became a calico cat. "Maybe. I've got unfinished business here in town. But I need your help."

Shaking his head, he glanced toward the door. "I'm not helping you catch the madam. You know I work part-time over at the saloon, cleaning up."

Hannah smiled, a flirtatious lifting of her lips. He'd always been sweet on her. "I know. You were nice to me when I was there."

The boy blushed, and she laid her hand on his arm, trying to remember what the women in the brothel had taught her about how to flirt and make a man feel wanted.

"It wasn't your fault you were forced into being a soiled dove."

"No, it wasn't," she said sweetly. "All I need you to do is get my supplies at the mercantile. You know I can't go in there." She pulled out the money Ruby had lent her until she could earn her own, along with a list. "Here's what I need."

"That's a lot for one person."

She leaned in close and whispered, "Don't say anything, but Jackson Colster is with me."

"The preacher?" he said, his eyes wide. "They told everyone he was dead."

"They nearly killed him. I'm taking care of him until he's strong enough to leave."

The boy frowned and shook his head. "He's a good man. He's just in the wrong town."

She glanced around the barn and took a quick peek outdoors to make sure no one was coming. "So will you get me some food and medicine? You could meet me down at Hodge Creek to give them to me tomorrow night."

If he didn't help her, she'd be forced to either ride to the next town or go into the mercantile herself. She knew she'd never make it back out of town without the madam's goons trying to stop her. Eventually, she would face them all, but for now she wanted the art of surprise on her side.

"Why do I think I'm going to regret this?" the boy asked. "Yes, I'll do it. But I'm not helping you get even with the madam. I need my job."

"Didn't expect you to." Hannah shrugged. "So what did my stepfather want?"

"Who?"

"That man who was just here. What did he want?"

The young man glanced down at his boots then back up at her. "He asked me to make sure his horse was ready to go early in the morning. He's leaving town."

She frowned. "Did he say where he was headed?"

"No. Just said he was leaving town in the morning. Wanted me to have his horse ready to ride, early."

Her forehead drew together, and she couldn't help but think about what there was possibly out of town that he would need. "If you learn anything about why he's leaving, I would appreciate knowing."

The boy kicked at the dirt. "You know he captured another girl and brought her to the madam? You heard about that, didn't you?"

"No, I'm kind of hiding out here. What happened?"

The boy sighed. "The preacher didn't tell you?"

"The preacher has been unconscious or in and out. He's not made much sense."

It wasn't entirely untrue, but she wanted to hear what Tim would tell her. Trusting everything the preacher said would be difficult.

"That's why they tried to kill him. He helped this girl that your stepfather had kidnapped escape. He got her a horse and helped her get out of town. Last I heard, they hadn't found her."

So the preacher had helped another girl, though he'd refused to help Hannah. While she was glad the girl got away, it only made her angrier than ever that he hadn't offered Hannah any assistance. Had he disliked her so much he'd ignored her pleas for aid?

And now she was stuck helping the damn man.

"If you learn anything at all about what my stepfather is doing, come tell me."

"How would I find you?"

"Just go to Hodge Creek and whistle. I'm around."

The boy gazed at her. "I know you've had your share of bad luck, but you look good wearing a gun. Do you know how to use it?"

She smiled, feeling proud of what she'd accomplished while she was gone. "That's what I was doing these last months. Learning how to protect myself."

~

Jackson ached all over. Sure, it had only been two days since the beating, but he didn't feel like he was getting any better. More bruises seemed to be popping up in places he didn't expect them. The mirror in the cabin showed the swelling in his eyes was beginning to go down, but his face was nothing but a rainbow of green, purple, and yellow.

But with each painful breath, he felt reassured he was still alive. He'd survived the goons and had even been rescued by a girl he'd turned his back on. For months, that day had haunted him. He'd been new in town, and though he'd known the town's reputation when he'd arrived, he hadn't expected to find it as bad as it was.

Bad enough he'd reconsidered what he was doing and even thought about returning home. But there was no home to go back to, and all he could do was stay here and try to clean up as much as he could.

The door to the cabin swung open, and in walked the woman he'd been thinking about. As a prostitute, he'd thought she was pretty, but now she was more like an avenging angel. Gorgeous with her reddish blonde hair tumbling about her shoulders, her green eyes flashing at him. He couldn't help but admire her.

"You're supposed to be resting," she said, carrying in her saddle.

"I am," he responded, "but I couldn't just lie here any longer. I'm slowly making my way to standing."

The sooner he got his strength back, the better. If the goons found out he was still alive, they would come after him and Hannah.

"Guess, I can't blame you for that," she said, piling her gear in the corner.

"Where did you go?"

"Into town to arrange for supplies."

Who in town could she trust to get them supplies? It couldn't be any of the soiled doves in the saloon. Who would help her?

"You didn't just ride into town, did you?" he asked, concerned that she'd put herself in danger.

"No, I know a boy I went to school with who's going to bring us food and medicine."

She certainly was pretty enough to turn a young man's head, but he'd be taking a huge risk helping her.

"Since you've been gone, where have you been, Hannah?" he asked.

"I've been learning how to protect myself," she said. "I've been learning how to shoot. I've been learning how to catch criminals and bring them to justice. But most of all, I've been getting stronger and stronger. I'm no longer that weak little girl who'd been given a bad blow. Now I'm a strong woman set on getting even."

He sighed. "I can understand why you'd want revenge. Your stepfather dealt you a woman's worst nightmare. But revenge is not going to make you feel better. It's not going to give you back the lost time in that brothel. It's only going to make you like them."

"Keep talking, preacher. Keep right on telling me that vengeance is the Lord's. Do whatever you have to do, to get your soul count in, but I'm promising you there will be bloodshed, and I will be right smack in the middle."

Jackson laid his head back against the pillow and closed his eyes. Hannah had every right to be angry with him and with the Lord. She'd been thrust into evil, and while she'd found a way out, he'd not been there to help her when she'd asked for his assistance. Once he'd learned the truth, he'd gone to the brothel only to learn she'd escaped.

At the time, he'd felt happy for her that she'd gotten out of her situation. But now she was back, and once again, Mrs. Hutchins was scouring the countryside for young girls to work in her depraved den of horrors.

"Who is Melissa?" Hannah asked suddenly. "You kept asking me if Melissa was okay."

He hung his head. "She was a young woman I helped." He'd been determined to make up for not rescuing Hannah, so when he'd learned of Melissa's fate, he'd done what he could to help get her out of town. The last he remembered, he was putting her on his horse and sending her on her way. Then the goons had caught up to him and everything else was a blur.

"Is she why they beat you up?"

"Yes," he said, wishing he had the courage to bring up the past and tell her he was sorry. "She worked in the brothel, and I helped her get away."

Hannah bristled like a porcupine; he could almost see the thorns come out. She turned to face him, placing her hands on her hips. "So you could help Melissa, but not me?"

He licked his lips, feeling nervous, shifting in the bed, trying to get comfortable. "I helped Melissa because I didn't help you. And I was wrong."

"Yes, you were," she said, turning away from him, giving him her back as she returned to putting up the supplies.

The madam had not only gotten him fired from his church by making certain his congregation believed that he, a single man, was visiting her establishment, she'd also framed him, and they'd believed her, not him.

"What about Melissa?" he asked, sitting up straighter in bed. "Did she get away?" Part of him didn't want to tell

Hannah, but another part knew she needed to know the truth. Last night, she'd saved him, brought him into this cabin, and was risking her life for him. The least he could do was be honest with Hannah and tell her about Melissa.

"She was a girl whose story is similar to yours," he said softly. "Only I didn't wait for her to approach me, I stole her from the brothel then set her free."

She stared at him. "Preacher man, there's a commandment against lying."

He couldn't blame her for not believing him. He'd refused to help her when she needed him the most. Now she thought he was lying about Melissa. "I deserve that and more from you. But why else do you think they were beating me? They were searching for Melissa. They wanted to know what I'd done with the girl. Unfortunately, her horse threw a shoe, and I let her ride my mustang out, hoping they wouldn't realize I was the one who helped her escape."

Nothing had gone as planned, and the girl had been frightened. She'd been warned that if she tried to escape, they would beat her, and from what he'd experienced at the hands of the madam's goons, he didn't know how a woman could take such a beating.

"You'll excuse me if I'm not jumping up and down and praising you for helping the poor young girls who are forced into being soiled doves. You didn't believe me, so I'm not certain this isn't some tale you think will keep me from kicking you out the door. Believe me, if those goons find you here, you're as good as dead."

And Hannah would be as good as dead as well.

"No. After you left town, I learned the truth about your situation."

"Even though I told you the truth that day."

He couldn't blame her for being angry with him because he hadn't believed her when she'd asked him for help. Even if she had been a soiled dove by choice, he should never have turned her away. He should have helped her get out of that life and introduced her to God. That was his calling, his faith, and he'd made a terrible mistake.

"Hannah, I was new to town. Wasn't even certain why the church had sent me here, but I'd just rolled in, and here you come telling me you'd been forced into working for the madam. I wondered why you just didn't walk away."

She laughed, the sound cold and eerie. "I did. Three times. And they promised me if I did it again, they would kill me. At that point, I didn't care."

She rifled through their supplies on the table. "Ruby was the only person who offered me any help. She kept promising me she'd get me out of town. Then my own lack of trust almost got me killed."

He watched her and knew that hidden deep within her was a caring person who had been forced to learn to be tough and trust no one. And how could he blame her. First her stepfather, then the madam, then the preacher—she'd been betrayed by everyone.

And yet, here she was taking care of one of the people who'd done her a lot of harm.

"I'm going to earn back your trust, Hannah," he said quietly.

"You're not going to be here long enough to earn back my trust. Not unless you plan on being here a thousand years because frankly, that's how long it's going to take to earn my respect again."

Chapter Three

"Thanks for doing this," Hannah said as Tim dismounted from his horse with her supplies at the creek's edge.

"Don't thank me just yet," he said. "The man at the mercantile kept asking me all kinds of questions about why I needed turpentine and camphor."

How could she risk Tim's life, yet she'd needed the medical supplies for Jackson's wounds and the food to restore her meager rations.

She frowned. "What did you tell him?"

"Told him I occasionally used the medicine on the horses in the stable. Seemed to shut him up for a while. Then he got curious as to why I was buying flour when he sees me at the diner every day."

"That old man is trying to cause trouble," she said, wishing she was just like any other woman and could walk into the store and purchase what she needed.

"Well, he's not the worst of your problems."

She stopped transferring the supplies from his saddle bags to hers and glanced at him. "What's wrong?"

"At the saloon last night, I overheard Mrs. Hutchins tell your stepfather that if he could find a blonde girl, that would be wonderful," the young man said, shaking his head as he watched her pack away the goods he'd brought.

Hannah froze as fear trickled down her spine and anger soared through her. "He's going to kidnap another girl."

"It would seem that way," Tim said, handing her the last of the packages.

"Did he leave this morning?"

He grinned, a mischievous smile that made her wonder. "Nope, his horse developed colic. But I can't do that forever."

"Did you make the horse sick?" Hannah asked, hoping he hadn't deliberately hurt the poor animal.

"No, I lied to Elliott."

"Why?"

"I thought you might want to go after him. Catch him in the act and turn him in," he said. "I couldn't get out here last night. I was afraid you'd think I was an intruder and shoot me."

She smiled at him, but not a full-blown womanly grin. Tim had a crush on her, and she wouldn't encourage the young man or give him false hope. Her experience with men was over. "I probably would have."

"So, his horse had a mild bellyache. I told him it would be better for him to leave the next morning. I thought his horse would be feeling better by then," the boy said with a chuckle.

Shaking her head at him, she laughed. "You can be devious."

Tim stuck his hands in his pockets. "It's not right, forcing girls into being soiled doves. If you chose that life, that's one thing, but no one should be obliged to work upstairs."

"Thanks, Tim," she said softly. "I'll be ready to follow him in the morning. Then I'll be back."

The young man lowered his head and glanced at the dirt, before looking up and staring at her. "You know my mother worked at the saloon before Mrs. Hutchins bought the place. I don't have a clue who my father was."

The news of Tim's parentage wasn't a surprise. In the little one-room schoolhouse in a small town, everyone knew everything about people.

She shrugged. "My father was killed when I was thirteen. Then my mother made the horrible mistake of marrying Elliott."

He nodded. "Life isn't easy for kids like us."

"No, it's not." She stepped back, afraid he was going to try to kiss her. "Thanks for bringing me the supplies. I better get back in there and check on the preacher man. While I'm gone, you might come out and see if he's okay."

Tim shuffled his feet, his hands still in his pockets. "I wish I could go with you, but I don't think I'd be any help. Be careful going after Elliott. You don't want to find yourself back working at the brothel."

She gritted her teeth and forced a smile. "Don't worry. There is no way I will ever return to the saloon, except to free the women who are trapped there."

~

When Hannah came into the cabin carrying her saddle bags with the pouches overflowing with supplies, Jackson lifted his head off the pillow, his body sending shooting pains ricocheting through him.

"You didn't go into town, did you?" he asked, fear clutching his sore middle. If the sheriff or the madam saw Hannah had returned to town, she'd disappear faster than cake at a church function.

"No. Tim from the livery stable brought this to me," she said, putting most of the supplies into the cabinets. The rest she packed neatly into the saddle bags.

"What are you doing?" he asked, watching her move about efficiently.

She turned and gazed at him, her emerald eyes not at all friendly. Even after a week of staying together in the cabin, she had warmed very little toward him. Even after he'd said "I'm sorry". But he couldn't blame her. If their roles had been reversed, he'd hate him as much as she did.

"Tim told me Elliott is leaving to go after another girl in the morning. I intend to follow him," she answered.

Anger rushed through him, and he clenched his fists in

the sheet, wishing he was strong enough to fight them again. He'd just taken a beating trying to keep a girl from prostitution; he wasn't going to let them just find another to take her place.

"No," he said, shaking his head, doubting this stubborn woman would listen to him, but knowing he had to stop her. "You can't go alone."

She gazed at him, her eyes boring a hole in the middle of his chest. "Who's going to go with me? You, preacher man? You can hardly get out of bed."

"Get me a horse. I'll go with you."

Shaking her head, she walked over and pulled out a pan. "I asked Tim to check on you while I'm gone. I'll be back as soon as I catch or kill Elliott."

Gripping the blanket, he wanted to jump out of bed and protest, but instead, he lay there, trying to rein in the fear and hurt that threatened to control him. "Hannah, I know you think I'm ignorant, but believe me, you don't want to kill your stepfather."

She turned and gave him a look that should have melted the blankets from the bed, her emerald eyes flashed with annoyance. "You don't want to kill the men that beat you senseless?"

"Of course I did at the time. But killing a man leaves scars. You wake up in the middle of the night and see his eyes. During the war, you think it could have been you. You wonder who they left behind."

Placing her hands on her hips, she glared at him. "Whereas, I wonder if someone had rescued me from this monster if I'd still be that innocent girl. I wonder about his next victim. How can I let him ruin another girl's life? I think about what I endured, and squeezing the trigger seems easy and feels satisfying."

Only for a split second, then his face reappears in your brain at the oddest times. And you wonder if you hadn't killed him, what kind of life he would have now, after the war? A young boy should never go to war. The emotional wounds left scars that ran so deep they only scabbed over and never went away.

Quickly, he pushed the thought away. Shaking his head, he said, "It won't change things. You'll still have the memories, but now you'll have blood on your hands."

"And you think he doesn't? My mother would never go into a bordello, yet she died at the bottom of the stairs. He said she slipped and fell. Lucky for him there were no witnesses. Or were there? Was he trying to force my mother into working upstairs and she fought him?"

Jackson watched her hands shake as she stared at him, her emerald gaze as cold as stone.

"Elliott Potter has a lot to answer for. Not only did he gamble away his money, but my mother's as well. You can preach all you want, but in the morning, I'm following Elliott out of town. And if I do my job right, he won't be returning."

She turned away from him to the fireplace and built a small fire. They were only using the fire to cook late at night and making certain it was out before dawn. They were close enough to town they both feared someone seeing smoke coming out of the chimney during the day. But after a week of hardtack, they'd had no choice but to cook some beans and bacon.

"So who did you kill?" she asked her back to him. He was surprised it'd taken her this long to ask.

A shudder rippled through him as the memory of that awful day came back to him. The smell of blood everywhere, the noise of cannons, the smoke, the screams, and he wanted to vomit.

He swallowed. "A young boy."

She whirled around and faced him, her body tense as she stared at him in the darkness of the cabin. Silence cloaked the small room, as she reached over and flipped the bacon in the frying pan.

There was so much pain and suffering swirling around them. Hurt that neither one had brought on themselves; they just needed some time to heal. Time to gather strength before they returned to the battle.

"Is there a wanted poster on you, preacher man? I need to know, since I'm a bounty hunter."

"No wanted poster," he said, not offering her more information, knowing she wouldn't ask.

"Good, because I would turn you in and collect the ransom."

He laughed, glad to see the atmosphere wasn't as charged with emotions as it had been. "I know you would, Hannah. If there's a price on my head, I don't have a chance. I'd have to surrender my beaten body to you."

She stood there with the fork in her hand and stared at him in the darkness. "Are you making fun of me?"

"Never," he whispered. "If you kill your stepfather, there will be bounty hunters looking for you. As far as I know, it's still against the law to kill an innocent man."

For a moment, he thought she was going to take the skillet and hit him with it. Turning back to the fire, she lifted the pan from the blaze then gazed at him like he was the stupidest person she'd ever met. "Who says he's innocent?"

"The law, until someone files charges against him."

"I know that. But I'm going to file a complaint when I take him in, unless he runs from me. Then I'll be thanking God and taking aim."

"What about the madam? What are you going to do with her?" he asked, shifting in the bed, trying to get off his wrapped, broken ribs.

"Oh, she's got no chance. I'm taking her business down. Makes no difference to me whether I take her in, or she tries to run, and I aim and fire. One less woman with a band of prostitutes."

Jackson knew she had every reason to feel anger, and probably here in this cabin was the best place for her to let some of that fury loose. But still, he could feel the desire for revenge radiating from her like heat from a stove, and he knew she had no idea what she was wishing for. Sure, she wanted them dead. He remembered the idealism he'd had when he'd thought about the war when he'd been so very young. But then, living with the reality was something he'd never forget.

"What about your church? Don't you want to get revenge?"

"God didn't turn his back on me. God's people turned their backs on me," he said, hearing the bitterness tinging his voice. "And when I tried to clear my name, my congregation didn't want to hear the truth."

She slid the crisp bacon and potatoes onto two plates, grabbed a couple of forks, and headed to the table.

Carefully, he slid from the bed. When his feet touched the ground, his vision spun crazily. He gripped the blanket around his privates with one hand and held onto the bed with the other. In a minute, the world quit shifting, and he took a step toward the table.

For the last two days, he'd lay in bed willing his body to heal, knowing his time was limited before they were found. He wanted to ride, and that started with this first step.

Turning around with his plate in her hand, she stopped. "What are you doing? You should stay in bed."

"No, I need to get stronger. Especially, if I'm going with you tomorrow."

"You're not. You would only slow me down."

"Come on, it's Elliott. How fast do you think he's going to ride? He'll be lucky to make it halfway to

Dyersville tomorrow."

"Maybe so, but you need to stay here and rest."

He paused as he walked very carefully from the bed to the table. He sank into the chair, making certain the blanket was still wrapped around him. Sure, she'd seen him naked, but that time he'd been hurt. Now he was bruised and achy and weaker than a newborn baby, but he still had some male dignity. Some pride still flowing in his veins that demanded he become stronger.

"I'm going to get better," he said, as the pain of that short walk radiated through him like he'd walked on hot coals. Even with the binding around his ribs, he was often short of breath.

Picking up his fork, he took a bite of the bacon and potatoes. After the hardtack he'd eaten for days, this tasted delicious. "This is good."

"Thanks," she said, focused on her food. "Why did your congregation turn their back on you?"

He stopped with his fork halfway to his mouth, realizing she had no idea about what had happened to him or what he'd done trying to change what he'd seen going on in town. She'd been gone when he was gathering his flock to fight the evil in their community. "I was caught with a prostitute."

She turned and gazed at him, but he couldn't see her eyes in the darkness. They still were not using a lantern, afraid someone would see the glow and wonder who was living in the shack.

He could tell his words shocked her, and it rankled him that just like his congregation she would believe he'd use one of the women for his own needs. The last time he'd lay with a woman was long before he'd become a minister. "It's not like it sounds. I did not have sex with that woman."

"Sure, you didn't. I can't tell you how many men from

your fine church I serviced on Saturday night, and then they went with their wife to listen to your sermon on Sunday morning. It just proves you're like all of them. I was beginning to think maybe you were different."

He reached out and grabbed her chin, pulling it so she had to look at him. "I *am* different. I wasn't having sex with that girl. I was trying to save her, since I didn't save you."

~

Jackson lay in bed, staring up at the ceiling in the darkness. He knew it was nearly morning, but since he'd been in bed every day, he was having more and more trouble sleeping all night. And when he wasn't dozing, his mind was busy thinking about what he could have done different. How could he get his congregation back, and did he really want to continue being a preacher?

Like the spinning of a wheel, his mind went in a thousand different directions, never lingering in one place for long. He loved his job. It wasn't the preaching so much as the interaction with people. Helping them when they were down, when they were sick, or when they just needed encouragement. His job as the leader of that small church was not to scream and tell them they were evil. Oh no, they knew they were sinners. His job was to hopefully show them a path that would help them lead a better life where they could spend eternity with their Lord and Savior.

At first he'd tried to ignore the saloon and whorehouse in town. After all, people always found a way to get what they need. But after he'd turned away Hannah and learned the truth, he knew he could no longer let that blight sit there on the horizon. In order to get rid of the situation, he had to clean up the town.

And so he'd begun the ugly task of trying to rid an

outlaw town of a crooked sheriff and a ruthless madam. Only, they'd won the first round. But now, he was more determined than ever to sweep the streets clean, and he'd call in the Calvary or the Texas Rangers if he had to.

A moan came from the floor, and he listened more intently. From being in such close proximity with her this past week, he knew Hannah often cried in her sleep. It was like when she lay dreaming, her guard was down, and sometimes she would weep or mumble.

"No," she called out, her words clear and distinctive this time. "Mother, no, no. You can't leave me."

The sound of her cries ripped at his heart. If only he hadn't been so stupid when she'd asked for his help. If only he'd believed her. He would have done his best to get her out of town, just like how he'd done for Melissa.

She thrashed around in the blankets. This dream was the worst one yet.

"Stop," she screamed, and he couldn't take it any longer.

He crawled out of bed, wrapping the blanket around him. He leaned down beside her on the floor and realized how cold it was down here. It was a wonder she'd hadn't become ill.

Gently, he touched her on the shoulder. "Hannah, wake up. It's only a dream."

She sobbed softly in her sleep, and his heart wrenched at the sound. Pushing a lock of hair away from her face, he stroked her cheek, feeling the soft skin while he cooed gently trying to wake her. The woman was beautiful, but she was a mess. On the outside, she was strong and tough as nails, but inside her soul was bruised and battered.

"Hannah, wake up. Everything's okay."

Suddenly, her body went stiff, and he knew she was awake.

She pushed his hand away from her face. "Don't touch

me. Stay away from me."

"I was only trying to rouse you. You were having a bad dream."

Her chest rose and fell in rapid short breaths like she'd been running a mile. He didn't dare tell her it had happened on more than one occasion. She yanked her blanket up to her neck.

She licked her lips and sat up. "I'm sorry I woke you. You can get back in bed now."

"It's okay. I was having a hard time sleeping."

The thought of crawling back into that empty bed again was less than inviting. He kind of liked sitting down here on the floor beside her, touching her, helping her wake from the world that frightened her.

Releasing a deep sigh, she laid her head back. "Sorry, I have dreams. Nightmares, and I just want them to go away."

He leaned against a table leg, keeping his blanket tight around him. "Sometimes it helps to talk about them. What are your dreams about?" Listening to the hell she'd gone through being a prostitute was not something he wanted to hear, but his duty as a man of God required him to council his flock.

She gave a little derogatory laugh. "Preacher man, that is something you really don't want to hear, unless it excites you."

Shrugging his shoulders, he tried to act like it meant nothing, knowing she was trying to shock him. "No, it doesn't excite me. But you mentioned your mother's name."

"Yeah, that's when it all started. Her dying and soon after, I found myself working for the madam."

He'd lost his mother when he was younger than her, so he knew a little something about loss. "I know you've suffered a lot, and if it helps you to talk about it, I'm here to listen to you."

"Well, thank you for being so willing to hear all the crap that happened to me at the bordello. If I ever want to talk, I'll be sure to find you. We can have a cup of tea, maybe even some cookies, and I'll confess what positions were the most popular among my clients."

"We can speak about whatever you want to discuss," he said softly in the darkness. "We might even find some scripture that shows how beautiful the physical side of love can be between a man and a woman." Somehow, he had to help her heal from those dark days and bring light and joy into her existence.

With a bitter laugh, she said, "You just don't give up, do you, preacher man."

"If I gave up at the first sign of trouble, who would take my place? The sheriff? The madam? No, I get discouraged, but I remember why I'm here on this earth, and I've decide I'm going make it as nice a place as I can, even if that means taking a beating."

Glancing at her in the darkness, he could feel her eyes on him and wished he could see her expression.

"You are a stubborn man."

"Of course I am. Wouldn't be here if I wasn't."

She grinned, and for the first time, he thought maybe they were getting somewhere. Maybe he'd put a chink in that wall she had around her heart.

"Why did you come here?" she asked. "If you could have gone anywhere in the world, why did you choose Hide Town, Texas?"

"That's easy. It chose me. I didn't choose it," he said. "Someone told me West Texas didn't have a preacher. They told me only those strong in their faith should consider this town. They almost presented it like a challenge. And here I am. Bloody, bruised, and still not ready to walk away.

Putting miles between him and his home in Georgia could only be a good thing. Too many memories of a young boy growing up during a turbulent time when defending a way of life meant duty to country, even if he'd been barely old enough to understand.

She yawned. "You know sometimes that could be considered stupidity, preacher. Stupidity and stubbornness sometimes go hand in hand.

"I guess we'll have to wait and see. Is that why you came back? Stupidity and stubbornness?"

"Oh no. It may seem brainless for me to return, but I can promise you my persistence will soon rule the day. If I have to die trying, I will get my revenge."

"And that's what scares me about you," he said in the darkness. "I'm afraid you'll be too obstinate to see that you need help cleaning up this town."

"Could be, preacher man."

~

The next morning, Hannah awoke just as the sun was rising. She'd overslept after talking into the night with Jackson. Ruby had told her that sometimes Hannah spoke in her sleep, but Jackson had said she cried. And that would explain why sometimes she awoke with her cheeks wet and her eyes red and swollen.

Quietly, she rose and pulled on the riding skirt Meg had fashioned for her. The practical garment had hidden pockets for her pistol, and she could ride astride a horse with no worries.

When she was ready to leave, she glanced over at the preacher in bed. After spending a week inside the cabin with him, she'd begun to think he wasn't half bad. Sure, he'd made a mistake by not helping her, and she'd yet to forgive him, but she'd at least acknowledge he wasn't a bad man.

"Hannah," he said, rising up suddenly in the bed. He swung his legs over the side. "I'm going with you."

"No," she said. "We've already discussed this, and you're staying here."

"We need to get me a horse."

The man was as stubborn and determined as they come, but she refused to back down. He had no business riding for long hours. Not after the beating he'd taken. And she didn't like the thought of him suffering even more. "No. I've got to go now, or I could lose his trail."

The preacher stood and she saw him sway. "You're not going. Now climb back in bed, and I'll see you soon."

His arms came around her, and he smashed her mouth against his. For a moment, she was stunned. The man was kissing her. His mouth was moving over hers in a way no one had ever done before. The feel of his lips against hers was nice, romantic, and even a little arousing.

Most men didn't kiss the whore they slept with. Most of them just wanted to stick their dick in your womb, and five minutes later, they were done.

Anger surged through her at the idea of Elliott getting away because she had been kissing Jackson.

She pushed Jackson away. "What are you doing?"

In the early dawn light, she could see his lips turn up in a smile.

"I'm kissing you goodbye."

"Well, don't," she said, stepping back. "And you're still not going with me."

"See you later, Hannah. We'll meet again."

She grabbed her saddle bags and marched out of the cabin, slamming the door behind her. It was time to go. To get away from Jackson. To leave him and the confusing feelings he wrought in her.

She reached up and touched her lips. The man could

kiss. She didn't know how he'd done it, but that kiss had felt nice. That kiss was scary.

Now was a good time to leave Jackson Colster.

Chapter Four

Every muscle in Jackson's body ached. And as much as he didn't want to admit it, he knew Hannah had been right. He had no business being on a horse riding after her.

After she'd left, he'd walked to town, rented a horse from the stable, and with Tim's help, he'd ridden out of Hide Town before anyone caught him. Now he was almost halfway to Dyersville, wishing he would just die, knowing he'd soon be forced to stop or fall out of the saddle.

The last streaks of the setting sun had disappeared, and all that guided him were the stars but still no sign of Hannah. It was dark, cold, and the last time he'd felt this bad was the night of the beating. Every muscle was screaming in agony for him to get off this plodding animal, but he was afraid if he dismounted, he could never climb up again.

The glow from a fire beckoned him, and he feared it would be Elliott's campfire. Slowly, he made his way toward the light. He groaned in satisfaction when he saw it was Hannah.

He rode his horse right into her camp, not stopping until he came to rest next to her fire. He slid out of the saddle as she stared at him in shock, her gun pointed at him.

"That's quite a welcome," he said, staring at her six-shooter. "Good to see you, too."

He swayed on his feet, the ground seeming to move of its own accord. He just wanted to lay down and be prone for a while.

"What are you doing here? Are you crazy?" She reached out to keep him from falling, and he took the opportunity to slant his mouth over hers again. Not that he had the strength, but just because he knew it irritated her, and he liked kissing her luscious mouth.

He hadn't realized how much he'd enjoy caressing her mouth until he'd done so that first time at the cabin. Then he'd only kissed her to make her agitated, but after the first time, he wanted to do it again. She was soft and tempting and oh-so gorgeous. He wondered what she'd been like before her stepfather had given her to the madam.

Even so, he liked Hannah. He liked her toughness. Her attitude. He knew one day she'd put her past behind her. Then the real woman would unfold like a butterfly.

She pulled back and gazed at him, her emerald eyes flashing with annoyance. "Have you lost your mind? A preacher doesn't kiss a whore. And you've kissed me twice now."

"Who says?" Jackson said, thinking his legs couldn't hold him much longer.

"I say so."

"I'm not a preacher anymore, and you're no longer a whore."

"Don't kiss me again," Hannah insisted.

"Oh, now you're just tempting me," he said, knowing he wanted to kiss her beautiful mouth again at the first opportunity.

"No, I'm not." She gazed at him. "Would you please sit before you fall down?"

He grinned, wishing he could argue more with her, but knowing he would soon collapse. "Oh Hannah, you do keep life entertaining."

She shook her head and led him over to the fire. "I told you to stay."

"And I told you I wasn't going to."

"So, do you still think following me was a good idea?"

A laugh escaped from his throat, and he leaned back on her blanket. "No. I may never move again, but I'm here."

Shaking her head, she pulled his blanket off the back of

his horse. "At least you had the good sense to bring your own blanket to sleep in."

"And supplies. I brought the supplies that were in the cabin." He hadn't wanted the madam's goons to find their stash and make off with Hannah's goods. Right now, it was the least he could do to help protect her. But soon, he'd be recovered, and he'd do whatever he had to, to save her from harm.

"You better not slow me down, preacher man, or I will leave you behind."

"Wouldn't expect anything less from you. But I wasn't going to let you go alone to try to stop an evil man." Right now, she didn't want to admit she needed help, but Hannah Williams was one small woman against an army of evil. She needed his help.

"I can do this," she said.

"Maybe you can, but I wanted to be here. I insist on helping you bring in this guy. It's not that I doubt your ability. But I let you down once, I want to make certain he doesn't harm another girl," he said softly.

Silence filled the camp as she stared at him. In the glow of the fire, it looked like she was smiling. Was she finally accepting him?

"Are you hungry?"

"Starved," he said. "But I need to rest."

Cleaning out her empty bowl, she filled it with a broth-looking liquid that had lumps of an unknown meat.

His stomach tightened and he swallowed. "What's that?"

"Jackrabbit stew. It's really good."

"How did you get the jackrabbit?"

"How do you think?"

"Oh."

"Eat the stew, you need it," she said, raising her brows at him like a mother would to a child.

He resisted the urge to stick his tongue out at her. With a sigh, he lifted the spoon to his lips, and after the first bite, he couldn't get enough. He didn't say another word until the stew was completely gone.

When he glanced up, she was smiling at him. The transformation of her lips turned up in a grin, her eyes glinting in the firelight, made her beautiful. Here, she seemed so much more relaxed, and the change was stunning.

He swallowed, trying to rein in the lust he could feel gathering like a storm in his loins. This wasn't good. "I think that's the first smile I've seen on your face. It's pretty in the moonlight."

"Don't flatter me, preacher. It won't get you anywhere."

He shrugged. "I'm just enjoying seeing you happy."

A coyote howled in the distance, the sound lonely. "Have you seen Elliott?"

"Not yet. I've been following some tracks, but I'm not certain they're his. We're halfway to Dyersville," she said, taking the bowl from him. Quickly, she wiped it out then cleaned the fork and spoon. In a matter of minutes, the dishes were done.

She threw another stick on the fire and piled up several branches ready to go into the flames.

Her movements were quick, precise, and he had no doubts she knew what she was doing. The woman seemed at ease here; whereas in town, she seemed guarded and jittery.

"We'll be back on the trail at daylight, following the tracks I hope are Elliott's. If not, we'll arrive in Dyersville without our man. I just hope he didn't make good time and arrive there too long before us."

"That could mean trouble," he said.

"Yes."

Gazing at her moving about the camp, he was surprised when she stopped in front of him. "I need my blanket back. I laid yours over on the other side of the fire."

While he appreciated her keeping distance between them, that lonely man inside him wanted her closer, longed to have her within touching range. But that wouldn't be good.

He patted the small Bible he carried in his shirt pocket to remind him of his faith.

"Were you afraid I was going to bite?"

Her gaze reflected her ire. "No. I'm not afraid of you or any other man."

"Then why so far away?"

"Because you're a preacher and I'm a woman who'll live without a man. Now, go to sleep."

"Has anyone ever told you, you're bossy?"

"No, you're the first. Thank you, now go to sleep."

Thank you? She was taking it as a compliment? He almost laughed, but suddenly he was too tired to even talk any longer. His body demanded rest, yet he occasionally gazed over at the woman who intrigued him. Hannah Williams was a much more complex woman than he'd given her credit for.

~

Elliott Potter was looking for a beautiful girl he could steal from her home and cart back to Hide Town. Part of him felt remorse at how a family would be missing a daughter, but if he wanted to survive and win the favor of the madam, he had no choice.

This would be his fifth girl-napping, and he knew soon he would need to travel further in order not to grab the attention of the law.

Riding into the darkened town of Dyersville, he

glanced around the small town and located the local saloon. First, he needed a drink. Then tomorrow, he would begin the search in earnest. He hoped to be back in Hide Town before Emily had a change of heart about going to dinner with him.

He knew the sheriff was sweet on her, but he'd love to push the lawman—if you could call him that—out of the picture. The two of them, Emily and him together, could do great things. With her money and his brains, they could create an empire.

After sliding off his horse, he quickly tied the animal to the hitching post and strolled through the saloon doors. Tonight, he just wanted to unwind and rest. He'd pushed hard to reach the town with hopes of getting back to Hide Town as soon as possible.

He swung onto a barstool. "Whiskey," he said to the bartender.

Closing his eyes, he rested for a minute before he opened them and glanced around the room at the odd assortment of men. He could tell so much about a town from the clients at the local watering hole. Here, you always got an indication of what types of people lived in the area.

"Thanks," he said then slammed back the alcohol. "Another."

"Boy, you must have had a terrible thirst," the man sitting beside him said.

"Yeah, you could say that, just rode into town."

"Staying long?" the young man of about twenty asked.

"Depends," he said vaguely, not willing to share too much information. "How 'bout you? You from around here?"

The fresh-faced kid smiled like he'd just won first prize at the county fair. "I live here. I'm getting married tomorrow."

"Congratulations."

"I'm pretty excited. My bride, she's over at the hotel. Once we say our I do's tomorrow, then we'll move out to our homestead. I can't wait to carry her over the threshold and make her mine," he said, beaming with excitement.

Elliott took a deep breath and wondered about the girl. Could she be the type of woman he was looking for?

"Bartender, another round," he said, wanting to get this kid so drunk he wouldn't know when his bride went missing.

"What's your name, son?"

"Adam Martin."

"Let me buy you a drink to celebrate your upcoming nuptials. Two more whiskeys, bartender."

The man behind the bar set the shot glasses in front of them. Elliott clinked his glass against the boy's. "To many happy years together, Adam."

The boy put the glass to his lips.

"Down it, boy. That's how a man drinks whiskey, and tomorrow you're going to be a husband. The man of the house."

The young kid grinned like he'd been handed a million dollars, but soon, he'd find out it was all fool's gold.

"What's your girl's name?"

Adam closed his eyes, like he was savoring her name. "Beth."

Nodding, Elliot said, "Tell me about the girl you're marrying. Is she pretty?"

"She's gorgeous. Blonde hair, blue eyes, and sweet as can be." The boy grinned and lowered his slurring voice. "You know I'm a little nervous about the wedding night. This will be a first for both of us. We wanted to wait until we'd said our vows."

A virgin. A blonde. She would bring in a lot of money.

He slapped the boy on the back. "You'll do just fine.

Sounds like you've got a great girl there. Bartender, another round."

"Oh no, that's enough," the boy said.

Elliot couldn't believe his good luck. It sounded like he'd hit the jackpot on his first night in town. It didn't get any better than this. Now to complete the deal. "No way. This is your last night of being a free man. We need to celebrate."

Elliott smiled. As soon as he could get the hotel room number from this kid, then the girl would be his. A little chloroform and he'd have a blonde virgin to put to work in the madam's brothel, his way into Emily's heart, and the empire she could help him build.

He whistled until the noisy saloon became silent. "Gents, this young man is getting married in the morning to a fair damsel named Beth. Raise your glasses in a toast."

"Hear, hear," some called and raised their glasses.

Soon the young man had free drinks flowing in front of him, and he didn't turn them away. When the midnight hour struck, the saloon began to wind down, and Elliott knew the time had come to put his plan into action.

"Adam, you look like you can hardly walk. Let's get you back to the hotel. I'll help you."

"Thanks," the boy slurred, barely able to hold up his head.

Oh, this kid was going to have one hell of a headache in the morning. Not to mention his wedding would be ruined. Elliott knew he should feel bad, but he didn't. The kid had brought his misfortune upon himself, and Elliott was there to reap the rewards.

He helped him off the bar stool, and together, they stumbled to the door.

"Good night, everyone," Adam called as they walked out of the saloon. He stopped and took a deep breath of the fresh air.

"What's your room number?" Elliott asked as they resumed crossing the street to the hotel.

"209."

They walked into the empty lobby.

"We should go serenade your girl."

The boy giggled. "I don't think she'd appreciate me waking her up in a drunken state. And I don't think the hotel management would like us disturbing the other guests. She's just across the hall, so I'll just blow her a kiss goodnight."

This was like stealing candy. Adam was making it so easy to find his girl. In some ways, Elliot pitied the young man. Tomorrow's hangover, losing his girl, and having his heart broken all in one fatal swoop.

Stumbling up the steps, they arrived at the boy's hotel room. "Big day tomorrow. Thanks for tonight, Elliott. I had a great time."

"Good luck with your wedding," he said and pushed the boy into the room and closed the door.

Hurrying back down the stairs, Elliott walked out of the hotel and went to prepare for the ride out of town. If everything went according to plan, he'd be on his way back to Hide Town in the morning with a girl who would make the madam a lot of money, a girl who would certainly win him favor with Emily.

~

Early in the pre-dawn hours before the roosters started crowing, Elliott went back to the hotel with his horse, prepared to make the capture. Sneaking up the back stairs of the lodge, he went to the girl's door and knocked quietly. He'd forgotten to ask, and he hoped she was alone.

She cracked open the door, and that was all he needed. Pushing his way inside, he quickly covered her mouth with a cloth that held chloroform to muffle her scream. She struggled for just a moment then passed out. Just like that, she was his.

Opening the door, he peered down the hall. No one was about. He lifted her onto his shoulder and carried her down the stairs. Once he reached the outdoors, he quickly tied her to the spare horse he'd brought.

Glancing up at the hotel where an unsuspecting young man was sleeping, waiting to awaken on his wedding day, he shook his head. "Better luck next time," he muttered to himself.

After climbing on his horse, he rode out of town, starting the two-day journey back to Hide Town, where he was certain Emily would be happy with the goods he was bringing her.

~

The sun had risen when Hannah and Jackson rode into Dyersville. The color in Jackson's face was better this morning. Yesterday, she'd been afraid for him when he'd rode into camp looking like an apparition barely sitting his horse.

A small part of her admired that he was so tough and determined, while her womanly part wanted him gone. He was dangerous, and she'd do best to remember he could only break her heart.

"Look over there," he said, pointing down the street. A crowd was gathered in front of the hotel. "Something's wrong."

The sheriff and a young man whose face was pale stood in front of the crowd. "Beth Gunderson has disappeared from her hotel room. She's missing, and we don't know why. Has anyone seen her?"

"When did she go missing?" a man in the back of the

crowd yelled.

"This morning."

Sitting astride their horses, Hannah and Jackson glanced at one another. She could see they were both thinking the same thing. Elliott had gotten here before them and had already done damage.

"Excuse me," Jackson said. "Have you seen a tall man with dark hair, green eyes with a scar above his eye? Did you see him in the hotel?"

The sheriff shook his head. "We checked everyone in the hotel. They're all accounted for."

"Wait," the young boy said. "Last night at the saloon, I met a man named Elliott. He had a scar above his left eye."

Hannah's heartbeat quickened. "What does your fiancée look like?"

The boy licked his lips. "She's blonde with blue eyes, about five feet tall and tiny." He closed his eyes and hung his head. "I had drinks last night with Elliott. Round after round of drinks until I was drunk. Said we were celebrating my last night as a single man. Then he helped me back to the hotel. I told him her room was right across the hall from mine."

Swallowing the fear that had risen up inside her like a sour stomach, Hannah ached for the young man. He'd been duped by Elliott and paid a heavy price. "When did you realize she was missing?"

"This morning, she didn't answer the knock on her door." He stared at them, looking confused. "How do you know him? Did he take her?"

Hannah glanced at Jackson, who nodded. "If he has her, he's going to sell her to a brothel in Hide Town. We've got to catch them before they reach town. He's got almost a half a day's ride on us, so we better get going."

"I'm going with you."

"I don't—"

"Hannah, he's lost the love of his life. He needs to go with us," Jackson said, softly touching her on the arm.

Tingles of awareness traveled through her, and she nodded.

While she hadn't wanted the kid to go for fear of him slowing them down, she felt a warm spot in her heart at the way Jackson had stood up for him. The young man did love this girl, and they needed to rescue her from Elliott and put her stepfather out of business once and for all.

Chapter Five

Hannah kept glancing at Jackson. His bruises were starting to fade, but she knew his ribs were still healing, and they were riding as fast as they could without hurting their horses. There was no time to stop and let Jackson rest. They had to ride quickly to save this young woman from a life she didn't deserve. Hannah worried if Jackson could keep up at this pace.

Before they'd ridden out of town, Hannah had found Elliott's tracks at the back of the hotel. She'd used the knowledge Ruby had taught her to see the direction the two horses had trotted off. Sure, it could be someone else's horse footprints, but she didn't think so. It was the same pattern of horse shoes she'd followed coming into town. Headed in the direction of Hide Town.

Now they were trying to catch up to her ruthless stepfather. And the poor boy, who was with them was struggling with a hangover, beside himself with worry. It was so refreshing to see a man who cared enough about his woman that he was going after her, fear etched on his face, determination locked in his jaw. She could see he was scared and unwavering and anxious beyond his dreams, but resolved he would get back the woman he loved.

Love. She'd never experienced the emotion, and part of her was jealous of the feelings he had for this girl. In her past life, she'd dreamed of a man loving her, but no more. No one would want a girl who'd slept with countless men, even if it had not been her choice. She was soiled goods, and it would be best if she separated herself from decent society.

"Look at that strip of cloth," Adam cried out. "That's part of her nightgown."

"She's leaving us clues," Hannah said. "We must be

getting close."

They'd been riding hard for several hours, and even Hannah was starting to feel the way the saddle bounced between her thighs, rubbing her raw.

Jackson rode well, but he had a determined glaze on his face. It was almost like he'd focused on the trail and nothing else. His complexion was pale, yet he too would not stop and rest until they'd rescued the young woman.

Less than an hour later, they came across another piece of material, and Hannah began to feel hope. Elliott and Beth couldn't be much further ahead.

As Hannah, Adam, and Jackson topped a rise, she could see two riders ahead. "There they are," she cried.

"I'm going to kill that son of a bitch," Adam said.

"No," Hannah said. "He's mine. You get your girl." She leaned low over her horse and kicked his sides.

"Hannah," Jackson screamed, but she wasn't about to listen to any more from him about forgiveness and thou shall not kill and all the other religious idealism that spouted from between his lips. She had a vengeance to settle.

Elliott Potter had kidnapped yet another girl, possibly killed Hannah's mother, and ruined her life. He wouldn't live to see another day, if she had her way. No judge, no jury, no trial. Her Colt six-shooter would do the sentencing.

With her horse galloping at full speed, she pulled the gun out of her holster, took aim, and fired. The bullet bounced in the dirt in front of Elliott. He whirled around to look at her and moved his horse in front of the girl, placing her in danger, keeping Hannah from shooting at him again.

There was no way she would risk the life of the girl, and there were other ways to reach Elliott.

Kicking the sides of her horse, she tried to catch them, but Elliott managed to keep the girl between him and Hannah. He knew she wanted him dead. He knew she'd kill him.

Finally, the girl realized what he was doing and slowed her horse. He turned around and barked something at her and pulled a gun, waving it toward her, moving just enough for Hannah to get a shot. She fired her weapon again, and this time she nicked him in the arm.

Screaming out in pain, he dropped his weapon and clutched his forearm. He glanced behind him and began to shout obscenities at the girl and Hannah.

When he no longer held a weapon, Beth pulled her horse to a stop.

Hannah raised her gun to finish him off, when Jackson rode up beside her and slapped her arm, almost knocking her from her horse.

"Stop!"

Like a storm, her insides exploded as fury rose inside her. She yanked on the reins of her horse, coming to a halt. She doubled up her fist and hit Jackson on the arm, trying to shove him off his horse. "Why did you do that? I could have shot him. He'd be dead now and wouldn't be able to harm anyone else."

"And you would have been a murderer. Is that what you want? To spend your life in prison or be hanged for killing your stepfather? You can't shoot a man in the back, even if he deserves it."

Tears clogged her throat as anger consumed her at the realization she could have shot Elliott. He would be dead if it weren't for Jackson. She blinked away the anger that threatened to spill from her eyelids at any moment. "What does it matter? My life is over. At least this way, I would have killed the person who hurt me."

"Because you're not like that," Jackson said his voice soft and gentle. "You don't see it, but you're kind, you care about people, you defend what's right. You're not a cold-blooded killer."

Closing her eyes, she bit her lip, her heart wrenching with pain. No, before, she'd never wanted vengeance, but that girl no longer existed. That girl had died those many months ago. Now, now, she ached with the urge to kill the people who had hurt her.

"You need your eyesight checked, preacher," she spat out before turning to the young woman who sat crying in her saddle.

Adam stopped his horse and jumped down. He dragged Beth off her horse and cradled her against his chest. "I'm so sorry. I thought I'd lost you forever."

Tears streamed down the cowboy's face, and Hannah swallowed hard to keep from crying with him.

The girl sobbed in his arms as she hugged him tightly. "You came after me. I was so scared."

Adam stroked her head, clutching her like he'd never let her go. "Of course I came after you. I love you. You're going to be my wife."

Jackson took Hannah's reins and turned her horse in the opposite direction. He led them a short distance away. "Let's give them some privacy."

Hannah yanked her reins back from Jackson. "We need to get away from here before we make camp for the night. I don't think he'll come back because I wounded him. But you never know. The man's wounded and vicious."

Jackson nodded. "And we will, once they have some time together. They're a sweet, young couple in love. Today was supposed to be their wedding day," he said in a soothing tone.

Why did rescuing this girl hurt so badly? Sure, Hannah felt joyous they'd set Beth free. Now she had her life back. She could marry, be a wife and mother, and live like a normal woman.

"Good for them," Hannah said and rode away, her heart heavy. She was glad they'd recovered the young woman, but part of her ached with sadness. Why hadn't someone saved her? Why couldn't she still be that innocent young woman yearning for love? Wanting someone like Adam to love her?

She'd spent months training for this split second, only to have Jackson ruin it. In her moment of triumph, he'd spoiled everything. But this was just a setback. She'd go after Elliott again, and when she caught him, she'd kill him.

~

Jackson couldn't watch her kill a man without trying to stop her. Yes, she had every reason in the world to wish him dead, but that didn't mean she should shoot him.

As the sun sank beneath the horizon, he gazed around at the camp they'd set up for the night. The young couple was sitting on the ground not far from him, their arms wrapped around each other, holding on like a united front nothing could separate. Hannah had given Beth a riding skirt and a shirt until they could get back to Dyersville.

Another pot of jackrabbit stew sat on the fire with Hannah stirring the pan, and he knew it wouldn't be long until they were eating mighty well…if she didn't poison his portion. He hoped to live to see another day. She'd been furious with him this afternoon, spitting fire mad he'd stopped her from killing Elliott.

And maybe she had every right to be enraged with Jackson. He'd taken the decision out of her hands, but he didn't really believe she would enjoy taking the life of a man, even one she hated.

She hadn't spoken a word since they'd made camp but gone about the task of fixing them all something to eat.

"Hannah," he said gently.

She turned toward him, her emerald gaze dark with

rage.

"I know you're angry with me," he said. "I just couldn't let you gun him down in cold blood."

"I've been waiting months to kill Elliott, and you stopped me."

"If you're going to be a bounty hunter, then you have to bring in the criminal, not shoot him dead." He couldn't stop himself from reaching out and touching her on the arm. His hand caressed the silky skin on her shoulder.

She stepped out of his reach. "As far as I know, he's not wanted. But that didn't stop me from wanting him dead."

More than anything, Jackson wished he could heal Hannah's hurts. He wanted to cleanse the pain from her heart and restore the girl she once was, so she could become the woman she was meant to be—a woman who was loving and kind, not filled with hate.

"Why haven't you gone to the sheriff and filed charges against him? Now there are two of you. If you both file complaints, he will be wanted. Then you can go after him, capture him, and bring him to justice."

"Who in Hide Town would believe me?" She sighed and clenched her fists. "I wanted to hurt him today. I wanted him to feel just a small amount of the pain I've endured. I wanted him to die."

"I know," Jackson said, touching her once again, rubbing his fingers along her arm. She was like a wounded animal, and he didn't know how to ease that pain with anything, except listening and caring. "You did a good thing today. You saved Beth from being sold into prostitution. You brought a couple back together. Now they can get married and start their lives without it being marred by the ugliness you suffered. You brought love together today."

Licking her lips, she glanced over at the young couple

sitting side by side, holding hands and whispering softly. Watching the couple, he felt the softening of her body, and for just a moment, she leaned her head against his shoulder as she stared at them.

"I'm happy for them."

Jackson sighed. At last, he could feel a peacefulness about her. "I know you are. Let's go talk to them about filing charges with the sheriff, so we can be certain Elliott is never capable of doing this again. Because you know if he gets away, he'll do it again," he warned. "Let's start with getting the law on our side."

"He's wounded, so I'm sure he's going back to Hide Town where he's safe. But you're right. We need to make certain he's wanted and everyone knows to be on the lookout for him in their town, so he can't do this again."

Jackson let his breath out slowly, feeling the tension drain from his body. Somehow she'd seen reason regarding Elliott, but Jackson didn't know for how long. He wasn't certain she wouldn't try to kill the man again.

Together, the two of them walked over to the young couple who were wrapped in each other's arms.

Hannah spoke with gentle authority. "I know the sheriff in Zenith. His sister-in-law trained me to be a bounty hunter. Jackson and I think we should go file charges against Elliott. If we both say we were kidnapped, then hopefully they will put out a wanted poster for him, and no other girls will suffer at his hands."

"There was also a third girl that we know of, Melissa," Jackson said. "I helped her get away, but I don't know where she's at. I'm hoping she's filed her own charge against him."

The two looked at each other. Then Adam said, "We could get married in Zenith and spend the night there after we filed the complaint."

The girl smiled shyly at him. "I like that idea. Then the

next morning, come back to our little place."

"If you'd like, I could marry you," Jackson offered. "I'm a preacher."

They both smiled at him. "I'd liked that," Adam said. "I think it's fitting."

Beth glanced at Hannah and Jackson. "In the morning, let's ride to Zenith."

~

Hannah introduced Jackson, Adam, and Beth to Zach as they stood in the sheriff's office. A shiver of fear clenched her insides, but she forced the emotion away. No longer would she let apprehension guide her life. No matter what the circumstance, she had to stand up and be strong.

"My stepfather, Elliott Potter, kidnapped Beth to sell her into prostitution. I'd gotten word he was going after another girl, and we followed him out of town. Then Beth came up missing in Dyersville. We'd both like to file charges against him."

Zach nodded and sat down behind his desk. He pulled out the necessary paperwork and began to fill it out, asking Hannah and Beth all kinds of questions, while Jackson and Adam stood in the background and watched.

When Zach had gotten everything he needed, he looked up from his writing. "I'll have this telegraphed to surrounding towns because he won't stop just because he's wounded. He'll be searching for another victim."

Maybe this would stop his sadistic hunt for young women. She didn't understand what was driving him to do such a terrible act. But whatever it was, he had to be stopped.

"On more pleasant news, this young couple was supposed to be married yesterday. Since that ceremony never happened, they'd like to get married today. I'm a preacher and can marry them. Is there some place in town where we can hold a ceremony?"

Just then, Meg opened the door and strolled in, her swollen belly preceding her. "Zach?" she called then saw the group of people. "Hannah, you're back."

"Not for long," she replied, giving her friend a hug. She quickly filled Meg in on what was going on.

Zach grinned at his wife. "Honey, this young couple wants to marry. Can you think of anywhere in town where Jackson could marry them?"

"Of course. They can get married at the farm. We'll all be witnesses. In fact, young lady, you need to come with me. We're going to find you a dress that will be perfect for the occasion."

"That's one of the things I love about my wife," Zach said, smiling with his loving gaze directed at his wife, "her take charge attitude."

The girl's eyes widened. "Thank you, but we could never impose."

Hannah knew exactly how the young woman felt. She'd thought the same thing. "The McKenzie women will love fussing over the two of you. You go with Meg. I'm going to ride out and speak to Ruby."

Now that Hannah had been out on her own for a while, she wanted to ask Ruby some questions and talk to her about almost killing Elliott and how Jackson had warned her about shooting him in the back.

Jackson's brows rose, but then he nodded toward her. She didn't need his permission to go somewhere, yet it was almost like he was telling her he understood. Their week spent together in that cabin had certainly made them attune to one another.

Meg took Beth by the arm. "I'm a dress designer. In fact, you're currently wearing a skirt I made for Hannah and my sisters."

"I love it. It's so easy to ride in."

"I saw the design in one of those New York magazines, and I knew I could do the same thing. Now come on, let's get you ready to marry that boy who is clearly infatuated with you."

The girl blushed. "I'm crazy in love with him."

Jackson grinned. "What time is the wedding?"

"Let's make it four o'clock at the farm. That will give us time to get Beth ready and gather everyone. Then you two can ride back into town and stay at the hotel."

Adam came over to Beth and gazed down at her. "Are you going to be okay?"

She smiled, lovingly staring up into her future husband's eyes. "I'll be fine. The next time I see you, we'll be standing in front of Jackson, saying our vows."

He grinned at her, his fingers reaching out to brush a strand of hair off her cheek. "See you soon."

Glancing at Meg, he said, "She'll be safe with you?"

Meg laughed. "I may be expecting, but I still know how to use a pistol. Honey, will Beth be safe with me?"

Zach shook his head. "I'd pity the fool who was stupid enough to take on my wife. We'll see you at the farm. You need to go arrange a hotel room and a ring."

~

Later that afternoon, Hannah stood with the rest of the people she called family and watched as Jackson wed the young couple. During the ceremony, Annabelle and Beau's daughter, Charlotte, started crying and Beau took her outside. The baby was six months old and her parents' pride and joy. Meg's baby was due the next month, and Zach doted on her. Ruby and Deke were also in attendance.

Hannah had spent the afternoon talking to Ruby about Hide Town and her stepfather. She'd confirmed what

Jackson had told Hannah. If she'd shot her stepfather in the back, it would have been considered murder. She guessed she owed Jackson a thank you, but the words had not spilled out from between her lips. They seemed stuck in her throat.

Watching Jackson perform the marriage ceremony cemented the fact that he was a preacher, a man of God, and though he was gorgeous as sin on Saturday night, they could never be. Until recently, he'd had a congregation where he was the pillar of strength, the person they all tried to emulate, and she would always be that soiled dove who'd escaped the madam, that poor soul who'd been sold into prostitution.

Not exactly church material. Yet, they seemed to have this thing developing between them she'd never experienced before. And that, frankly, frightened her almost as much as taking the madam down.

"By the power invested in me, I now pronounce you man and wife," Jackson said, jerking Hannah out of her musings.

She watched as Adam brushed back Beth's hair and kissed his bride tenderly on the lips. For a moment, Hannah felt envious. She'd never have a man look at her that way. She'd never have a husband or a family. All of that had been taken from her the moment Elliott had given her to the madam.

Biting her lip, Hannah concentrated on the wedding. Today, Beth looked beautiful dressed in a blue muslin dress Meg had had in her shop. She'd given Beth the dress as a wedding gift and asked her to send new customers Meg's way. Just like she'd given Hannah the skirt she was wearing.

The McKenzie women were strong and helped people achieve their dreams. She owed her life to this family, and she'd do whatever she had to, to protect them. Yet, she envied the life they had. Loving husbands, babies, and an unbreakable sisterly bond, everything Hannah would never have.

Annabelle stood. "Give me just a few moments, and I'll have supper on the table. We can celebrate this couple's new beginning."

Caroline McKenzie, their cousin, jumped up almost knocking over the oil lamp. "I'll help Annabelle."

Meg tried to go in and help too but was quickly shooed out of the kitchen by Ruby and Hannah. "Go sit down before you go into labor. Today is not the day we're having that baby."

With a laugh, Meg returned to the rocking chair.

"Come on," Ruby said to Hannah. "I need some space from Caroline. She's acting a bit crazy today. Her mother is pushing her to marry that pig farmer, and she's almost foaming at the mouth with anger."

Hannah chuckled at the idea of Caroline and the pig farmer. The woman's mother had been pushing the man toward her daughter for months now. "Has she gotten any better at shooting?"

"Yes, I think she can handle her own now, but I hope she never goes out alone. That mother of hers doesn't realize it, but she's pushing Caroline right out the door."

"At least she still has a mother who cares."

"What's wrong with you? You're acting sad, and you should be joyous."

Hannah shook her head, knowing she would never do anything to mar the young couple's day. "It's nothing."

How could she whine about her life when she was now a free woman? No, this wasn't the life she'd chosen, but she was independent, strong, and would soon get the revenge she craved. No, it wasn't a perfect life, but she was no longer working in a profession she'd hated, and that made it a good day.

"You know, Hannah, in the last six months I've learned to read that pretty face of yours. To someone who knows you, those expressions can easily be deciphered," Ruby said, smiling at Hannah like she knew exactly what she was experiencing.

"Well, let's keep this beautiful occasion focused on this couple. I'm so happy we found Beth before the madam got her."

"And you should feel proud you were the one who saved her."

"I am. I just wish someone had rescued me."

"Hey, I rescued you."

Hannah laid her head on Ruby's shoulder. "And I will be forever grateful."

Time would heal her wounds, and soon she would be making enough money to live on her own. She had to keep repeating that mantra over and over to herself.

Ruby sighed. "I know you wished it had been sooner, but you're still that beautiful young girl who one day is going to be standing before everyone saying I do."

"Oh, no," Hannah said, shaking her head. "No man is going to want to marry a soiled dove."

"You know, I thought you were a lot keener than that. I've been watching that preacher, and he can hardly keep his eyes off you."

Hannah turned and stared at Ruby. "Jackson? That would work as well as tying a bobcat with a string. Me, an ex-whore, with a preacher man? I'm sure his church would fire Jackson faster than a deacon taking up a collection on Sunday morning. Besides, he's not interested in me. He feels guilty because he didn't believe me and never helped me escape. That will soon pass."

The sun was blazing a hole in Ruby's brain, if she thought Jackson was interested in Hannah. Sure, he'd kissed her, but that was more to irritate her than being serious. And yes, they seemed to have this urgent need to be together, but that would end once they were no longer together for any length of time. Then they'd go back to just being a man and a woman who solved crimes together.

Ruby shrugged her shoulders. "Maybe so, but the only time I've ever seen a man look at a woman like he gazes at you is when he wants her in his bed."

"That's not happening."

Leaning in close to Hannah, Ruby lowered her voice. "You know, with the right man, sex is beautiful. You've been exposed to the worst side of the physical act, but when you're with the man you love, it's very enjoyable. Let's just say Deke knows how to make a woman sing."

Hannah shook her head at her friend. "And I'm sure your husband would be very embarrassed to hear you tell me about his bedroom capabilities."

Ruby put her arm through Hannah's. "There is not much I can do or say that embarrasses my husband. He knows exactly who he married, and he wouldn't have it any other way."

~

Later that evening, they all gathered outside to tell the young couple goodbye, and Beth hugged Hannah close to her.

"Thank you. Because of you, I'm back with Adam, and we're married. I can never repay you for what you've done."

Tears gathered in the corners of Hannah's eyes. "I'm just glad we found you."

As the couple prepared to leave, they promised to visit the McKenzies once they were settled. At first, Hannah had experienced guilt for wishing someone had saved her from Elliott's clutches, but after Beth's sweet thank you, she'd felt a rush of happiness that she'd helped someone. The McKenzie sisters had told her she'd done a good job, and they were proud of how they'd taught her to be a bounty hunter.

Now, Hannah knew it was time to get serious once again about Hide Town.

Jackson came up beside her. "That was what you call a happy ending."

"Yes," she said, watching the newlyweds ride away and avoiding eye contact with Jackson.

"You still mad at me?"

"Damn straight. But I talked to Ruby, and she said you were right. I would have been charged with murder for shooting him in the back. Thanks." Those words were so hard to say, yet they needed to be out in the open.

Jackson grinned at her and even gave her a brief hug. "Don't get discouraged. We'll get, Elliott. I've been talking to Zach about how to clean up the town. I've made a decision."

She glanced at him, trickles of worry going through her. "What?"

"I'm going back to my congregation. I'm reclaiming my church."

"Jackson, I don't think that's a good idea." The thought of him going back to those people who hadn't supported him and the men who'd nearly beaten him to death frightened her.

He smiled and wiped a piece of her hair away from her cheek. "It's what I've got to do."

"You're still hurting. Let's just go back and hide out in the cabin until you're well. We can make that our headquarters and return there whenever we run into a problem." She didn't know if his body could handle the torture if they beat him again. No matter what, she didn't want him hurt.

"No. I want to be out in the open, where they know I'm coming for them."

"Do you want to die?"

"No, but I'm not going to be a coward, and I'm going to fight for what's mine."

Uneasiness scurried along her spine. She'd begun to think of them as a team, and he was making the decisions. She had her own battles to fight in Hide Town, and this time she would win. "What about me?"

"You're going with me. We're going to clean up the town, together."

Zach walked up to them. "Sorry to interrupt, but we're getting ready to leave, and I wanted to give this to Hannah."

He handed her a wanted poster. "When I filed the complaint on your stepfather and sent out my telegrams, I received a message back from a sheriff in East Texas. It seems your stepfather is wanted for murder. He killed his first wife."

Hannah cursed. "I knew it. I knew he murdered my mother, and the madam helped him cover it up. They said she fell down the stairs, but why would my mother be in the bordello? No one would listen to me." Fury rushed through her, leaving her shaking.

Yes, it was time to return to Hide Town, and though she wasn't certain, maybe the time had come to quit skulking about and get on with the battle.

Hannah glanced at Jackson. "We leave at daylight to return to Hide Town."

Chapter Six

Hannah worriedly glanced behind her at the sky. Dark clouds roiled in the west, like boiling water, changing from light blue to almost purple. Springtime in Texas was often filled with storms as the weather changed from cool to hot, just like the way people went from warm to cold when they learned of her past.

"There's a thunderstorm brewing behind us. I think maybe we should bed down here for the night and hope the rain travels north of us," Hannah said, riding alongside Jackson.

He gazed at the rapidly moving clouds. "We're directly in the rainstorm's path. We're going to get wet."

A semi-circle grove of trees came into view. They wouldn't be under the trees, but at least they might get some help with blocking the blowing dust and wind. Trees were scarce upon the prairie, and when you found some, it was wise to take advantage of their shelter.

Riding into the center, Hannah pulled her horse to a stop and slid down from the animal. "I'll get a fire started."

Jackson stepped off his horse and gazed at the clouds for a few minutes. From inside his saddlebags, he pulled an oil-skinned tarp. "I'll build a lean-to to shelter us during the storm."

"If we get wet, we'll dry out."

"Not with wet wood we won't," he said.

She watched as he scouted around the area until he found branches he could use to create the cover.

The idea of being snug in a cramped space with Jackson was not exactly her idea of fun, but she hated storms. The power of them roaring across the prairie, where they had very little shelter, frightened her. About the time she got the firewood gathered, thunder rumbled in the distance. Lightning streaked the sky.

"Oh dear," Hannah said, her nerves skittering down her spine at the dominance of nature.

Within minutes, she had a fire roaring, while the clouds grew darker and the wind began to pick up, whipping the flames. Jackson immediately kicked dust onto the fire, extinguishing the blaze.

"Why did you do that?" she asked, looking stunned.

"Because I don't want to start a prairie fire."

"You're right," she said with a sigh.

"Put the wood you collected under the tarp," he said. "We'll need a fire to dry off after the storm passes."

After stacking their firewood inside the shelter, she stood. A gust of wind slammed into Hannah, and Jackson caught her.

A bolt of lightning hit the ground less than a hundred yards from them. She screamed and wrapped her arms around him, her body shaking. "I hate lightning."

"Shh, it's okay," he said, patting her on the back, his body surrounding and protecting her. He held her in the safety of his arms while tremors rattled her bones. In his embrace, a sense of safety and belonging overcame her. Something she'd experienced very seldom in her life.

"It's starting to rain. Get beneath the tarp." He'd tried to make it like a lean-to, but it would be barely big enough for the two of them laying inside.

She crawled beneath the covering, while the wind tore at the stakes in the ground. "What about you?"

"I'm coming. Let me make certain the horses are secure, and I'll be there."

She waited beneath the tarp, barely able to peek out.

"Here it comes," he said, crawling in just as the storm unleashed its fury on them.

Rain pummeled the tarp, and Hannah knew without it, they would have been soaked to the skin. Lightning flashed, lighting up the dark sky, and she whimpered.

Sitting on the ground beside her, Jackson wrapped her tightly in his arms. "It's okay. We need the rain."

"We don't need the lightning."

Hail plunked on the ground in front of them. At first, it was little pieces, and then they got bigger.

"Lay down," he ordered.

Fear clutched her chest as she lay on the ground. Ice pieces pounded the lean-to, bouncing around them. The tarp sagged under the weight, and Jackson covered her body with his, taking the beating through the tarp, which now sagged under the weight of the water and ice.

"I'm just trying to protect you from the hail," he said, his breath whispery soft against her cheek.

"I know, but you're the one recovering from a beating. I should be on top," she said, her body trembling as the storm raged outside. She could feel his taut abdomen, his sinewy thighs, his muscled chest, and thick forearms covering her. "Thank you."

Guilt filled her at the thought of his bruised and battered body covering her own, protecting her, while he got pounded through the oil-skinned tarp. Yet, he felt good laying on top of her. Too good.

He glanced down at her, and she could see his brown eyes glittering in the semi-darkness. "Miss Williams, I must tell you that your pistol is poking me in a very intimate place."

It was so unexpected that she gazed up at him and started laughing, releasing the fear and worry she'd felt only moments before. She'd never been out on the prairie in a storm. This was a first, and she was relieved she wasn't alone. "I'm afraid if I try to move it, I'll shoot one of us."

"That wouldn't be good, would it," he said, gazing down at her, staring at her in a way that was creating all kinds of nice cozy feelings soaring through her.

"No," she whispered, her lungs laboring for air. Beneath the tarp, she felt warm, secure, something she'd never experienced before. She gazed up at Jackson's full lips and licked her own. She'd enjoyed his kisses very much the other day, and this felt like the perfect place for him to kiss her again, but he was just staring at her like she was lunch, and he wanted what was on the menu.

Her mouth moved toward his of its own accord. She didn't tell her lips to go there, yet she wanted to taste him again. To feel his caress once more.

Tentatively, she pressed her lips to his. He didn't need any further encouragement. His mouth covered hers in a blazing kiss that seared her all the way to her toes. His hands gripped her face as his lips consumed her. She tensed beneath him as the sound of thunder rumbled in the ground beneath them.

He lifted his head, staring down at her. "If you want me to stop, tell me."

Oh my. She didn't want him to stop. She wanted more of these feelings he was creating inside her.

He captured her mouth to his once again, and she eagerly met him. That was the confusing part. She didn't want him to stop. At the time she'd been a soiled dove, most clients hadn't kissed her, and the ones that had had never felt like this. Never had her heart raced in her chest, her breath faltered in her lungs, or this warmth heated her center. This feeling he evoked was completely new to her.

His lips ravished her. She opened her mouth, accepting his unspoken acknowledgement of passion between them as his mouth plundered hers, voracious and demanding.

Her mind fought against the hunger she could feel growing inside her. She arched into him, feeling his hardened shaft nestled between her legs.

Like the storm outside, fear flooded her, swamping her desire. What was she doing?

"Stop," she said, pushing him away, her breathing heavy.

He gazed at her, and she could see the longing reflected in his gaze and feel the rapidness of his breath and the hardened desire snuggled between her legs.

"I'm sorry. I can't," she said, glancing away, fear almost choking her as the rain now hit the tarp with a soft, steady rhythm. "Your good book is poking me in the chest."

His fingers pushed the hair from her face. "Don't apologize, Hannah. It's okay. You make me forget myself. I guess God was sending us both a message."

"I don't need his message."

"We all need his message." With a deep sigh, he turned and glanced outside. "I think the storm outside has just about passed."

Need radiated from his body, yet he'd done what she'd asked. He'd stopped when asked, though he was hard with wanting.

Shock filled her as he rose from covering her and strode from the lean-to.

~

Riding the long, green prairie trail back to Hide Town, Jackson knew this time destiny would be fulfilled. Spring was a time of new growth, and he was determined the townspeople would soon experience the change the new season brought. His fate was to help Hannah clean up the town.

Whatever happened, whether he lived or died in the coming battle, he wanted Hannah to be safe. If Jackson was harmed or killed, Zach had promised he would find her. Jackson knew the sheriff of Hide Town would be searching for a way to end Jackson's days without the citizens aware he was gone.

Kissing Hannah during the storm last night had been a huge mistake. He'd suffered greatly from her soft womanly curves beneath him, her sweet mouth, and the way she'd gazed at him when she asked him to stop.

The woman was a temptation he'd never experienced. He longed to protect her, guide her, and comfort her. And yet, because of his own lack of courage, he barely had the right to ask for her name.

Hurt radiated from her soul, calling out to him. She was like a wounded animal frightened and injured, and he wanted to ease her damaged spirit. To make her whole once again. To be like a soothing, healing balm.

Yet, the thoughts he'd been having in that lean-to were more of a man who lusted after the woman beneath him. As a preacher, women threw themselves at him or arranged for their daughters to meet him, and not one had ever filled him with longing like Hannah. None of them had ever needed him like Hannah.

But she was filled with hate and a determination to kill and until she realized how hollow and painful those feelings were, he could never be with her. His heart ached with the knowledge of just how ugly that reality could leave a person.

Hannah remained quiet as they rode the prairie in the morning sun, heading for Hide Town. The citizens may be captive now, but Jackson had every intention of freeing the city from the outlaws that held it hostage and turning the city into a prosperous commerce, if he didn't die in the battle for justice.

On the edge of town, he turned to look at Hannah. "I'm not skulking in that cabin again."

She whirled in her saddle to face him, her eyes large and wide filled with fear. "You have to."

The thought of another beating caused his chest to ache with the fresh memory, yet he refused to hide away any longer.

"No," he raised his chin and faced her with determination. "We're riding into town. It's Sunday. I'm returning to my church. I'm getting my congregation back on my side."

"They'll kill us."

"I don't think so." He said a quick prayer, hoping he was right.

"And if you're wrong, we're both dead."

"Have faith, Hannah."

Spurring his horse, he rode through the middle of Main Street with Hannah at his side. People stopped and stared as if they were seeing a ghost. They'd believed he was dead.

Music spilled from the church at the end of the street. Halting in front of the building, he slid from his horse. Then he placed his hands around Hannah's waist and helped her from her mare. He liked the way she fit in his arms—her small, compact body snug against his own.

"Preacher man, I hope you know what you're doing," she said, shaking her head, gazing up at him like he was in need of a nuthouse. "I'm afraid, but I'm going to protect you."

He smiled. "It's Sunday morning. We need to be in church. The Lord will protect us."

"My six-shooter will lend him some help."

Taking her arm, he led her up the stairs of the building. He opened the door and escorted her down the small aisle, a smile plastered on his lips.

The Song-leader's face blanched, and he stopped, his mouth hanging open.

Jackson enjoyed the shock on the people's faces as he strode up the aisle to the pulpit, where he'd preached to his flock every week. He was back.

Releasing Hannah's arm, he pointed for her to take a seat in the front row. He walked to the pulpit, wondering who would shoot him first, and pulled his Bible from his pocket. "Thank you for that fine song-leading, George, but you can take a seat now."

An elder in the church stood up. "Jackson, we don't want any trouble."

Jackson motioned for him to sit. "It's a beautiful Sunday morning to celebrate life here in the Lord's house." He glanced around at the people staring at him, their faces drawn and filled with fright. "I know many of you believed the stories you heard about me. Believed I was consorting with a young soiled dove. Maybe you even believed I was dead and thought good riddance, he got what he had coming. But I'm here to tell you the facts."

Silence filled the vestibule of the small church, and he glanced at Hannah, drawing strength from the sight of her. "I've returned to do what Jesus did. Clean the temple. Only I'll be cleaning the town. We have lawless people running our community. The madam of the whorehouse is having young, sixteen-year-old girls kidnapped and forced into prostitution. At first, I didn't believe it when it was brought to my attention. But when Hannah escaped and then Melissa was brought in as her replacement, I knew what was happening. Some of you have young women in your homes. What if your daughter was taken?"

The people were staring at him in horror at the thought of their own women and children being captured. He smiled as they were listening. "I helped Melissa escape.

Because of that, I was beaten by the madam's goons and left for dead. Hannah rescued me."

There was a gasp, and one of the elders yelled, "You're still consorting with prostitutes!"

"You're right, and so are some of you. I know there are men in this very congregation who are going up to that brothel, using women. Some of you have family members who are probably wanted by the law. It's time to clean up this town." He paused, letting his words resonate. "I will be helping Hannah do just that. She's a bounty hunter. She's here to arrest the man who kidnapped her, who she thinks killed her mother. I'm going to help her any way I can. It's my goal to make this community a safe place for good people to live."

There was silence. He was trying to warn his congregation that life in Hyde Town was about to change. No longer would outlaws freely roam the streets. And if they had family members, they needed to warn them to get out of town. "If you want me to leave, I will, but if you're ready to make this a town worthy of raising your children in, then please stand."

For a moment, he could see them glancing at one another as if asking who would stand first. Finally, a woman stood and then another and another. Soon almost everyone stood. Several men were yanked to their feet by their wives.

Smiling triumphantly, he motioned for the Song-leader to return to the podium. "George, lead us in another song and a prayer for safekeeping this week."

As he walked back down the aisle of the church, many people reached out and shook his hand. Happiness filled his chest, as he realized he was back where he belonged, filled with the purpose of his mission for this church. When he reached the back of the vestibule, he gazed up at the stained glass cross that filled the back wall. The sun shone brightly through the mosaic, much like the determination beaming through him.

He hadn't turned his back on God. God's people had turned their backs on him, but he'd persevered, and now he was more unwavering than ever to meet the challenge head-on. His bruises were fading, his strength was returning, and his will felt like a hundred pound gorilla.

In the front row, he saw the soft red-blonde curls of Hannah. His heart warmed, and his loins tightened. The girl was a danger for him to be around, yet he felt responsible for her safety. She was a menace to herself, and he felt the need to protect her.

But could he take care of her, clean up the town, and save his congregation?

Chapter Seven

Hannah sat on the hard wooden front pew of the church, while everyone walked out, leaving her alone in the small building. No one had approached her. No one.

Her chest ached with the pain of being rejected, and she willed the hurt away.

Regardless of what Jackson had told them, they still considered her that soiled dove who'd been with countless men. How many more women were in that brothel feeling like they had no choice, no place to go, and no one who would want them?

She sighed, took a deep breath, and stood. Yes, people obviously thought she no longer belonged in polite society, but she had a purpose. A job to do.

She would find her mother's killer and bring him to justice—dead or alive, she didn't really care—and in the process, make the madam pay for how she'd treated Hannah. If possible, shut her down.

Glancing around Jackson's now empty church, she knew this was where he belonged and not with her by his side. Those moments spent together beneath the tarp yesterday were best forgotten.

Anger coursed through her veins. If there was a God, why had He forsaken her? She'd been a young, innocent victim, and He'd turned his back on her. She was happy Jackson had saved Melissa, but why couldn't it have been her? Why hadn't someone realized she hadn't chosen this life?

Raising her fist at the cross, she turned and walked away.

When she stepped outside, she saw Jackson talking to a crowd of people. He was smiling, laughing, and she realized she needed to slip back to the abandoned cabin on the edge of town. There, she could go about her business of finding her stepfather and freeing all the madam's girls. The time had come for her and Jackson to separate, yet that thought left her lonely.

Turning away from him, she saw the madam and two of her goons approaching. Her heart skipped a beat then swelled in her throat, racing like a pack of wild animals were chasing her. She wanted to run, but instead, she let her hand drop down to rest on the gun slung low on her waist. Her training kicking in.

"Hannah," the madam called, walking toward her with the two henchmen at her side, a parasol shading her.

She waited until the woman stood in front of her before she responded. "Mrs. Hutchins," she said, a sneer in her voice. There was no way she was going to let them take her. She'd die before she went back to work in the saloon.

"You've returned," the madam said. "You must have enjoyed working for me to come back to Hide Town."

"I hate you and your brothel," Hannah said, trying to keep from reaching out and scratching the woman's eyes out.

Suddenly, Hannah realized the crowd behind her had quieted, and she felt Jackson step up beside her.

"What's going on?" he asked.

"You're back, Reverend," Mrs. Hutchins said, laughing at him. "Which one of my girls do you want to spend time with now?"

"I rescued a girl from you and in the process, almost died, thanks to you and your goons," Jackson said, his voice steely.

"You look perfectly fine to me," the woman said, twirling her parasol. "I think Clara has been pining for you."

"Clara doesn't even know me," he said. "What do you want?"

"This girl owes me money. She's coming with me," the woman said, her voice stern. She motioned for the closest goon to grab Hannah.

Hannah whipped out her six-shooter and pointed it at the man. "Do you really want to die today?"

He hesitated.

"Please give me an excuse to kill someone," Hannah said, the gun pointed steadily at the madam. "I don't owe you a dime. It's not my fault my stepfather was in arrears with you. I should never have been made to pay for his debts."

"Oh, honey, he didn't owe me money. He made money selling you to me," she said with a laugh. "But you owe me for the room and board. The dress. The training."

Hannah felt like her world had suddenly tilted on its axis. All this time, they'd made her believe she had no choice but to pay her stepfather's debts, when actually he'd been paid for selling her to the madam.

Rage consumed her, making her almost blind with hatred. If Elliot had been there in front of her, she would have filled him so full of holes, he would never float.

"It's back to the brothel for you," Mrs. Hutchins said, smiling with a gleam in her eye.

The goon made to grab Hannah, and she cocked the hammer back on her gun. "Come any closer and you're a dead man. I don't owe her a dime. She stole my innocence."

"You heard Hannah. She's not going back," Jackson asserted, his voice filled with quiet strength. "We don't want trouble. But I have a crowd of witnesses. We're no longer going to accept you enslaving women. I'd suggest you get on down the street, unless you want a fight on your hands. Do you understand me?"

Hannah watched the woman glancing back and forth between the two of them like she was determining her next move. Jackson wanted Hannah not to kill anyone, but right now, she was shaking with the urge to pull the trigger on the woman who had forced her into a life she hated.

"Preacher Colster, you are stepping in a pile of manure you don't want to get involved in. I will crush you and take Hannah," Mrs. Hutchins said calmly.

"That may be so, but today, we have the firepower, and I know Hannah is just itching to kill you. So unless you're ready to die, I think maybe you need to mosey on back down the street."

Jackson understood Hannah, better than any person she'd ever met. He knew she was just aching with the need to kill the woman who'd prostituted her, but she'd reined in her first response because of him.

The goon stepped toward Jackson, and Hannah fired the gun at his feet. He jumped and the crowd cried out.

"Don't!" Hannah cried. "This man is just recovering from the beating you gave him. That was your last warning. The next bullet is hitting flesh, yours or the madam's, I don't really care."

Tension oozed from Hannah, and she could hear the crowd mumbling.

Mrs. Hutchins smiled and shook her head. "You may have the upper hand today, but it won't always be this way, Hannah. And when you're back at the brothel, you'll be punished."

"I'll die before I return to that place."

Mrs. Hutchins turned and walked away, taking her muscle-bound henchmen with her. Hannah watched her until she entered the saloon. Then she slid her gun back in its holster.

She turned to Jackson. "I'm leaving."

He frowned. "Where are you going?"

She didn't want to tell him. She didn't want to tell anyone. She only wanted to slip back to that little shack, where she had watched the town and prepared for the battle she knew was coming. Once again, she wanted to hide there until she was ready to take the next step. "You know where I'm going."

Jackson grabbed her by the arm. "There's no way I'm going to let you sleep out in that cabin by yourself. They know you're back, and they're going to be looking for you. If you're out there, they'll find you."

And they would. But she'd be prepared. She'd be ready and would take care of them right there. Not with an audience around, but slowly and methodically. "I'll deal with it."

"Stay with me. I have a house here in town," he said softly.

Her chest ached. Staying with Jackson sounded heavenly, but there were so many reasons why she shouldn't, including the fact no one would approve of the two of them alone.

"I'm sure your parishioners are going to agree to that," she said sarcastically. "Not a one of them spoke to me in church, the hypocrites."

When would she learn not to let people's opinions matter? But still, being totally rejected had left her feeling like a complete outcast. And now tears swelled behind her lids and filled her throat. She wanted to get away and nurse her wounds in private.

"Give them time. They had to accept a lot today, and they're still reeling from the fact I'm back and I defended both you and Melissa."

"I can take care of myself. I don't need them, and I don't need you. I'm the only person I can trust to look after me," she said, raising her chin defiantly.

In the past months, she'd learned to take care of herself. In fact, frankly, her life was better off without men.

"I understand." He glanced back at the people who

were now talking animatedly amongst themselves. "I'll find a widow woman to stay with us. That way my parishioners are happy. Your reputation is safe—"

Pain swelled in her chest, and she started laughing, the sound both sarcastic and sad. Quickly, she stopped before the tears flowed down her cheeks. She couldn't let these people see her cry. No one could ever know the depth of the hurt she felt when ordinary people refused to speak to her because of her past. "My reputation is beyond repair."

"No, it's not. We'll do things within society's boundaries, which will show your character."

She shook her head. "Preacher, it's your reputation you're worried about. You're talking about letting a known soiled dove live in your house. People aren't going to believe I'm not there servicing you."

They were being watched. The crowd of parishioners was observing them; she could feel their eyes on her, judging.

"Hannah, I don't care. You can't go back out to that cabin. If you insist, I'm going with you. Then I will be fired. Let me find a widow woman to move in until this is all resolved and you're free."

There was no way she wanted to let the madam to get her clutches on her again. She had her stepfather to find, and she had to figure out a way to shut the madam down. Being with Jackson would be safer for her body, but what about her heart?

The man could kiss the spots off a pig and make it shine. He'd had her body yearning for things she'd never imagined longing for again, and now he wanted them to live under the same roof?

No matter which way she turned, she could be hurt again. Maybe having an extra gun under the same roof was not such a bad thing. The two of them could better handle the situation in town; now people knew they'd returned.

And his congregation knew he'd only use his gun as a last resort. Besides, she'd only be here until this ended, and then she'd be free to earn a living as a bounty hunter.

"Okay, find a widow woman who will live with an ex-soiled dove under your roof. But frankly, I think you're going to have a hard time finding a woman who'll stay in the same house as me."

He smiled and stepped closer to her. "I know the perfect woman."

~

Later that evening, Jackson stared across the dinner table at the widow Margaret Schreiner. A member of his church, she was about the strictest sourpuss he'd ever met. She'd been a school teacher until she'd retired shortly before her husband passed away. Her reputation for being a stickler concerning rules was well known in his church, and he thought she would be the perfect chaperone to convince his congregation that nothing improper was going on in his home.

The woman wore her hair in a bun on top of her head; her dress was black with a high collar and long sleeves. A brooch was the only spot of color on the woman, and her expression could be just as dark as her clothing.

Margaret stared at the two of them, her hands together in a prayerful position. "Not only do I have the reverend's reputation to uphold, but my own. So there won't be any hanky-panky while I'm here, are we clear?"

Jackson laughed, but Hannah continued to eat her dinner. It was their first sit-down meal since they'd left the McKenzie's farm, and he could see the tense lines on her face. Today had been difficult for Hannah, first his congregation then the madam.

He didn't know how to make things easier for Hannah,

and he had to make certain she was safe. The thought of something happening to her was frightening.

"Mrs. Schreiner, that's the reason I chose you. I knew you would make certain I did nothing to hurt Hannah's reputation."

Hannah looked up from her supper, one brow raised. "I don't think you can damage mine much more. Besides, once this business is taken care of, I'm leaving town and starting over somewhere fresh to get away from the hypocrites."

How could he blame her? The memory of everything that had happened here was uppermost in her mind. In some ways it reminded him of how he'd been when he'd returned from the war—a young kid who felt like he'd seen the worst of humanity and never wanted to witness killing again. Yet here he was in a wild western town where shootings occurred almost daily.

"Hannah, I'm sorry my congregation wasn't more welcoming. They were barely civil to me. You've got to give them time."

"Hrmph," she responded.

"They're worried about their daughters," Margaret said. "If it happened to you, it could happen to them. They'll come around." The woman reached out and patted Hannah on the hand.

Hannah glanced down at the woman's hand then up to her face, her eyes narrowing like she didn't believe the woman was touching her.

"Have you ever lived anywhere else?" he asked, hoping to divert a fight.

Hannah looked at him and sighed. "No, my mother's family was from Mineral Wells, but I grew up on a small ranch just outside of town," she said. "My father, Seth Williams, raised cattle. Mother had a large garden."

Margaret smiled at the young woman. "I remember

your mother. I was so shocked when she died in that brothel. I couldn't imagine a nice woman like her going into a place like that."

Jackson spoke up, trying to thwart Hannah getting angry at Margaret. "We don't think she went in there. We think Elliott murdered her, then carried her body inside and placed it at the bottom of the stairs."

"My mother would not have gone in there willingly," Hannah said, the rage surfacing quietly.

Reaching across the table, Margaret touched Hannah on the arm again, and Jackson feared Hannah was about to unleash a torrent of anger on the older woman. She stared at Margaret, her gaze heated with fury.

"Dear, you've been through quite a lot in your young life. I'm going to try to help you clear your good name, and we start by making certain everyone knows you and the preacher are not together. I think we should sleep in the same room."

Jackson watched as Hannah's jaw twitched, and with relief, he realized she was trying not to laugh.

"That's fine."

"We'll have to share a bed. I'm such a light sleeper I'll know for certain you're in bed with me every night."

The expression on Hannah's face was almost priceless. She had one of those *I can't believe this is happening* looks on her sweet face. But there were still serious things they needed to discuss.

"Where else would I be?" Hannah said with amusement.

Jackson pulled out two guns and laid them on the table. "I know Hannah carries at least one gun with her if not two. But Margaret, I'd like you to wear one as well. For protection."

The woman's brows rose, and she tilted her head, narrowing her eyes at him like she'd probably done to all the misbehaving children in school. "I refuse to carry a weapon."

Why did Jackson feel like he'd brought the two stubbornest women the state of Texas had to offer into his home? Both of these women had wills of iron, and if someone did break in, he'd run like the hounds of hell were chasing him, after dealing with these ladies.

"Suit yourself, but I'm warning you. They're going to come after us, and while I have several men from the church who are checking on us hourly and will sound an alarm if we need help, I'd rather you had at least a little protection."

Hannah nodded her head. "I'm good. My weapons are never far from me."

Margaret shook her head. "I haven't carried a gun since the days of the Indian attacks."

"Well, now might be the time to consider your safety and carry one. I'm going to put this other one in the chest next to the good book. If you need a weapon, remember it's here. Margaret, this one is yours. Leave it by your night stand if you need to."

Suddenly, the sound of glass shattering had them all diving under the table, as a large rock flew through the front window and rolled across the wooden floor.

Jackson felt his heart pounding in his chest as he made certain the women were safely under the table. He'd known they would attack. He'd known they'd not let his return go unpunished.

"Stay down," he yelled.

Crawling on his hands and knees over to the rock, he picked it up and found a note. "Get out of town," he read.

"Good grief, did anyone invite the Baptist to town?" Margaret said jokingly, sitting under the table.

There was a pounding on the door. "Reverend, are you okay?"

Hannah yanked her gun out of her holster and stood behind the door. The reverend opened it, his gun in his hand. "We're fine. Did you see who threw the rock?"

The man shook his head. "No, but a rider galloped away. Do you want to go after him?"

"Yes, but you've got to stay here with the women."

"I won't leave until you get back. I'll wait here outside the door," the man offered.

Jackson knew they wanted Hannah to return to the brothel. He feared they thought by kidnapping her again her spirit would be broken, he would back off cleaning up the town, and once again, they'd be in control. But not this time. He would do everything he could to end the corruption in this wayward village and return it to the prosperity they'd once had.

He walked over to Hannah, who had crawled beneath the window and was peering out into the darkness. Grabbing her by the arm, he pulled her to her feet, putting a wall in between them and the window.

"I'm going to go out and look for that rider. I'm not going far," he said, staring into her green eyes. She was so pretty, and she didn't even realize the extent of her beauty. No wonder the madam wanted her back.

"I'm going with you. What if it's a trap?"

"No. I want you to stay here with Margaret. I'll have some men with me in case it's a trap.." She was staring up at him with such innocent eyes. And he wondered what she would have been like if none of this had happened to her.

Her mouth was full and ripe and so tempting. He glanced around to see the chaperone had walked into the kitchen. Quickly, he pulled her mouth to his and kissed her sweet lips. He moved his mouth over hers, needing to taste her one more time just in case this was his last few minutes on earth.

Heat spread through his body straight to his loins.

Fear of Margaret walking in on them had him breaking apart from her. "I've got to go. They're waiting on me. Don't leave the house. Stay in here with Margaret. I'll be back soon."

She grabbed him, pulled him to her, and kissed him one more time, then pushed him away. "Don't get killed."

He grinned. She'd kissed him. She'd initiated the kiss, and desire spiraled through him like a West Texas dust storm, swirling and covering everything.

"I don't plan on it."

~

Hannah blew out all the lamps, casting the house in darkness.

Margaret took a seat on the couch in the main room. "I guess we wait."

Standing next to the side of the window, Hannah peered through the glass pane that wasn't broken. Nothing was moving outside, and while she knew that was good, she wished she could see something that would let her know that either Jackson was safe or they'd found whoever had tried to scare them tonight.

What a cowardly act. To throw a rock through a window while they were nearby at the dining room table.

"You know my husband used to know your father," Margaret said in the darkness. "I didn't realize it until you mentioned him at dinner tonight."

"Really?" Hannah asked. "How did he know him?" She loved to hear tales about her father and his business. He'd been such a big, strong man, and his death had devastated her mother and ruined their ranch.

"They traded cattle. My husband had our herd outside of town. We lived here in the city. I taught school, and he tended our ranch business. Funny, in those days, there were less than a hundred people living here in town. We didn't even have a sheriff. Not until Mrs. Hutchins purchased the saloon and opened up the brothel upstairs."

For a moment, Hannah tried to imagine the town without a sheriff or a brothel. But they were far enough away from a major city that it was more of a frontier justice than a constitutional government.

"Why would a small town allow her to take over?"

"Didn't really have much choice. She came into town one day and bought out the saloon. The next thing we knew she had talked the town council into getting a sheriff."

Hannah glanced back out into the darkness. Nothing stirred. Whoever had frightened them tonight was long gone.

"You know Jackson is sweet on you," the woman said.

Hannah turned around and stared at the woman. She couldn't see her face in the gloom, but she knew she was still there. "Jackson is a nice man, but I'm not exactly preacher's wife material or really acceptable for any man."

She didn't need to hear this. She didn't want her feelings for Jackson to grow into anything more than what she felt already, for fear of being hurt. He needed a woman who could help with his church, and an ex-whore hardly fit the description.

"Why not? I bet you could help teach our younger men and women about the evils of the saloon and the brothel. You could help young women understand why it's important to learn how to protect themselves."

Hannah shook her head. Why waste your time on things that could never happen, when you'd only get disappointed when it didn't come to pass? She'd only get hurt, and she didn't know how much more devastation she could take in her life. "I'm not cut out to be a preacher's wife. God and I aren't exactly on speaking terms right now." She paused then asked, "What did I ever do to Him for Him to do this to me?"

Her hands started to shake, and she could feel the tears welling up inside her. "This morning in the church, not a soul spoke to me. I was ostracized. Jackson on the other hand is a good man; he doesn't need to be saddled with a wife who would only bring shame on him. He deserves a good woman who would work with him. I'd tell his congregation to go to hell."

Margaret laughed. "Lord, you do like to give me the toughest cases, don't you." She stopped laughing then said in the dark. "I'd tell some of his congregation to go to hell as well. We may just do it together."

Chapter Eight

Later that night, Jackson came back to the house and found the two women waiting for him in the dark.

"Any luck?" Hannah asked.

"No, he disappeared," he answered.

"Right into the saloon," Margaret said.

Unfortunately, Jackson feared she was right. If he took a guess on who had frightened them tonight, he'd say it was one of Mrs. Hutchins' goons. They were the ones who had motive to want them out of town. And sometimes he thought Hannah had the right idea.

Maybe he should just pack up and leave, but then he remembered the other options the church had given him and how he suspected they knew that this location would either make him a fine preacher or send him running.

"I'll talk to the sheriff tomorrow," Jackson said, stretching, trying to ease the pain in his side. He still wasn't completely healed from the beating.

He glanced at Hannah, who was watching him with those all-knowing eyes of hers. Now they had another kiss between them, another moment that had left them both breathless.

"Why don't you get some rest? I don't think they'll bother us again tonight," she said. "I can stay up and keep watch if you want me to."

"No, the men in the church are checking on us, so I think we'll be all right. I think we should all turn in and try to sleep."

Margaret didn't move. She stood there in the living area, glancing between the two of them. It took Jackson a moment or two to realize she was waiting for them to each go to their rooms before she retired.

Hannah grasped it as well. Shaking her head, she

glanced at them and said, "I'm going to bed. Good night."

"I'm right behind you," Jackson said, turning toward his room. He couldn't wait to sleep in his own bed for the first time in weeks.

"Reverend, a word with you please," Margaret said.

Her voice was commanding, and he halted and faced the retired school teacher, like a naughty boy. She waited until Hannah had shut the bedroom door before she walked to him. "That girl needs our help. She's angry, and well, I just feel so badly for her. We need to do everything we can to assist her."

"I'm trying, Margaret. Time is going to be the best healer. That and helping her put her past behind her. But until we capture her stepfather, there is no moving forward."

The woman nodded. "I can't blame her for feeling angry. She had a nice family. She's lost so much."

Jackson hadn't known Hannah's mother, but learning her family had lived here for years had opened his eyes. And that fact made him even more ashamed of how his congregation had treated her, but he'd soon deal with them.

"Yes, she has," he said, wondering where this conversation was headed.

Margaret placed her hand on her chest. "I'm here as long as you need me, Reverend, but you know, one way to win acceptance for her and to help that girl would be for you to marry Hannah."

Jackson had to bite his tongue to keep from laughing out loud. *Marry Hannah?*

"She needs a husband. And you're just the man who could help her start her life over. I know you want a family. She needs a family. I think it's the perfect solution."

If only Margaret would keep her mouth shut and not bring up ideas that were floating in Jackson's brain already. He didn't want to think about it right now. "Margaret, I appreciate the thought you're putting into helping Hannah, but she may not want to get married. Right now, I think she pretty much hates all men."

She shook her head. "Hannah wants you to believe she hates all men. And that's why you would be perfect for her. You could help her overcome that fear. Learn to love again," she said, growing more enthusiastic about the subject. "I'm going to get to work on planning something that would show her you are courting her."

Oh no, he liked Hannah, he really did. Probably way more than he'd anticipated, but to actively court her was not something he was ready to do.

He shook his head. "Right now may not be the best time. Let's wait until after the town is cleaned up."

Margaret was off and running with her idea whether he wanted Hannah or not, not listening to a word he was saying, and while the idea made him nervous, he wasn't completely immune to the idea of Hannah becoming his wife.

"We could hold a dance or a barbeque. I think I'm going to start taking her with me to the ladies' church functions. You know our teas. I mean after all, if you married her, she'd be our pastor's wife."

Somehow the idea of Hannah as a pastor's wife struck him as funny, and he could no longer contain his laughter. "Margaret, I like Hannah. I think she's suffered a lot, but to make her my wife…" He let the thought resonate through him.

It wasn't a bad idea, but still, he wasn't ready to consider that possibility. "I'm not prepared to take that leap just yet. Right now, I pray we all live through the night then get through the next few days. Don't plan a wedding when I'm not certain about asking for the girl's hand. Let's see what tomorrow brings."

She placed her hands on her hips. "Now, Jackson, I see

the way you look at that young woman. You need a wife, and she needs a husband."

"True, but I'm not ready to commit to anything," he said. "Good night, Margaret." He turned and walked out of the room.

Hannah was beautiful. She had a sweet spirit that had almost been destroyed. She needed time to heal. She needed the chance to be a young woman who found joy in living once again.

And he wasn't certain he could heal her need to maim and kill the people who had harmed her.

~

The next morning, after telling Margaret and Hannah to stay at the house and to keep their weapons handy, Jackson walked across the street to the church. He needed to look at the paperwork on his desk, see what letters he'd received, and began next Sunday's lesson plan. He had things to do with his church, besides cleaning up the town.

He'd been working for almost an hour, when he heard the door to the church open. He opened his desk drawer for easy access to the gun he'd placed there. While he hoped the good Lord kept him safe while he was in church, he had added a little firepower just in case the need arose.

The sheriff walked into his office. "Good morning, Reverend."

"Good morning," he said, leaving the drawer open. He didn't trust the man, and while he didn't believe the sheriff would shoot him here in the church, he wasn't taking any risks.

"How can I help you?" Jackson said, not standing or inviting the other man to sit. Frankly, he wanted the sheriff to leave as soon as possible. He didn't know why he was here. They didn't have much in common, so he could walk out the door right this moment, and Jackson wouldn't be upset.

The man sprawled his large body in the chair on the other side of Jackson's desk. "I heard you were back in town and just wanted to come by and say hello."

"Funny, I was going to come see you later this afternoon. Seems someone threw a welcome back rock through the window of my home with a message. They want me to leave town."

A belly laugh exploded from the sheriff. "Who would want you to leave our fair city?"

Jackson knew the sheriff was making fun of him, but he didn't care. When you were the only law in town, it was justice for all. But in Hide Town, that didn't exist.

"The first two who come to mind are you and the madam."

The man's brows raised. "Me? I think our town needs a preacher. You know someone to bury troublemakers. Send them on their final journey from this world to the next. Some people in town need the good book, but know their place in our community. You need to learn your place if you want to continue living here."

The warning was subtle but there nonetheless. But Jackson was tired of veiled warnings and threats and needed the sheriff to understand that yes, there would be a change but not his kind of change.

"What about preachers who are tired of seeing good, honest, hard-working people abused and want to end the violence in their town? Clean up the streets and make things right?"

"You mean troublemakers," he said. "Troublemakers are not allowed in this town. They receive one, maybe two warnings, and the third time, they need you, Reverend," he said, his dark eyes fierce.

Jackson sat back in his chair, raised his head, and met

the man's stare. The warning was obvious, but he didn't care. He was no longer going to live with what he saw. Before, he'd been willing to turn his head. He'd been new to town; he had been learning how things worked, but now knowledge was power.

"You know, this town has lived with bad influences for many years. I understand people just let things slide. They had family members that were wanted by the law, and they knew they could live here and wouldn't be bothered. But when Mrs. Hutchins took over the town, things changed. When women are forced into working in her bordello, there's a problem. A problem that can no longer be ignored," Jackson said, gazing at the sheriff.

The man's face was starting to turn red like he was getting angry that Jackson was being frank with him.

"And just what are you, the Reverend, going to do about it? It's not like you're fast with a gun. I'm still the sheriff in this town."

With a laugh, Jackson smiled at him. "No, but I have the power of the people behind me. They know about Melissa. They know about Hannah, but do they know about you, Sheriff? Do they realize you and Mrs. Hutchins work together? Do they realize she's paying Elliott to bring in young women? Do they know he's wanted for murder of his first wife and now his second wife has died mysteriously? I think not. But they soon will."

The man's eyes grew large and darkened. His face was stony, and Jackson knew if he hadn't been the sheriff's enemy before, he certainly was now. But he didn't care. The time for this ruthless man to end his tyrannical hold on the town was now.

"What are you going to do? Talk me into a jail cell? From my side of the desk, you're sounding like a troublemaker. And you know what I do with people who cause problems in town."

Jackson smiled and shrugged his shoulders. "No, I'm going to turn the people on you. From the pulpit, I'm going to form an army to clean up this town. There's nothing like religious people with a reason to seek justice."

"Preacher man, you may think you've got this all figured out, but don't be so sure. There's still five days between now and Sunday. A lot can happen in that time."

A trickle of warning spiraled down Jackson's spine. This man was dangerous, and he could harm a lot of people in his church. Innocents who just wanted to see justice done.

"That's why my congregation has already started. They're forming a first line of defense now. We're not waiting for Sunday to get here. We're already at work."

The sheriff's eyes narrowed. "When people start getting killed, I'm going to blame all of this on you, preacher man."

"You do that, Sheriff. Now if you'll excuse me, I've got things to do. Clean up your act, Sheriff, or suffer the consequences."

"I'm not worried." The sheriff stood. Kicking his chair out of his way, he walked to the entrance of the church. "You're a troublemaker, preacher. Your days are numbered."

~

Hannah knew Jackson had told her to stay in the house, but she couldn't. She needed to get out, to show the people in town and herself she was really seriously doing something to avenge her name and find her mother's killer.

With the wanted poster in her hand, she walked to the sheriff's office. Most people's eyes widened when they saw her. Some people from church nervously nodded their heads in greeting but didn't say anything. Everyone hurried past her. She felt like the woman with a scarlet letter on her dress.

Holding her head high, she walked right up to the sheriff's office. A faded poster that looked like it had been hanging there since the office was built still hung on the wall, but nothing new. Obviously, no one wanted to know who was wanted in this town and who was not.

Pulling some nails from her pocket and the small hammer, she unfurled the paper and begin to hammer it into the wall. A crowd of people formed behind her to see what she was putting up.

"Who's that?" someone in the crowd asked.

A gasp came from the front. "That's Elliott Potter. Oh my God, he killed his first wife? And Mary Williams died in the brothel."

Hannah turned around. "She was murdered as well. And I plan on proving it."

"He's here in our town. Any decent woman could be in danger."

"Elliott's a threat to society. He kidnaps young girls and sells them into prostitution. I don't have the wanted poster on that just yet, but there are two charges filed against him, including mine."

Hopefully Zach would send them the wanted poster as soon as it arrived. Maybe he'd even bring it to them, though she doubted he would leave Meg's side until their baby was born. She couldn't blame him for being with his wife when their firstborn came into the world.

"Why hasn't the law arrested him?" a man called.

"Ask the sheriff," Hannah said, watching as the lawman walked up the street.

The crowd was on him, yelling, asking questions.

He held up his hand. "What are you doing?"

"I'm hanging a wanted poster of Elliott Potter. He's wanted for the murder of his first wife and also for questioning with regards to the death of my mother." Uneasiness raced up Hannah's spine, as she faced the worst sheriff she'd ever met, one who didn't believe in upholding the law or the Constitution. He was a sham who worked for the madam.

"Your mother was a whore just like you."

The urge to reach for her gun was overwhelming, but she knew that would only hurt herself, not the sheriff. "My mother was a genteel lady who Elliott stole from. Then he sold me into prostitution, and I aim to get restitution."

"That's a fancy word coming from a girl who makes her living on her back."

His words were meant to be vulgar, to make her feel cheap, and it worked. But she refused to let him see just how much they hurt.

"I wasn't a whore until you turned your back on their unlawful activities, forcing me into prostitution. But now I'm a bounty hunter." She lifted her head, stiffening her spine, determined to no longer accept bad treatment from anyone—male, female, or even a whole congregation of so-called churchgoing people. No one had the right to make her feel bad about herself any longer.

Hannah would no longer be a victim. If she was going to die, she'd go down guns blazing and fighting every step of the way.

"I'm not here to try to convince young women to stay home and not make a living as a soiled dove. You chose the profession."

"I will collect on Elliott. You can tell him I'm here searching for him, and when I find him, he's wanted dead or alive."

The sheriff frowned. "I think you still owe Mrs. Hutchins money. I should haul you back down there to work it off."

Jackson came up behind her. "Discussion over. She's

not working for Mrs. Hutchins again. And we will be arresting Elliott once we find him. It's your duty as sheriff to uphold the law. This will be your opportunity to show us if you're truly a lawman or just a vigilante."

Jackson took hold of Hannah's arm. "Good day, Sheriff."

With a grip on her elbow, he walked them away from the gathering crowd. When they were a far enough distance that no one could hear them, he said in the strongest tone of voice she'd ever heard him use. "What were you thinking? Do you want to get forced back into working for the madam? Do you want to be killed?"

"No. I just couldn't sit in that house another minute, not doing something to change things. I had to get out. Besides, I'm used to working alone. I don't need you."

She'd never seen Jackson angry before, but his face was red, and his eyes were wide, shooting imaginary daggers.

"Honey," he said sarcastically, drawing the word out. "Everyone needs somebody. I know you think you're tough and strong and you can take this on by yourself, but you can't. You need some help. I need some help."

"I'm a trained bounty hunter. I can do this job."

"And I'm a preacher, and I still need help. It's not bad to need other people."

She turned to face him, tears welling up in her eyes, all the anger she'd held back rushing at her like a giant bolder crashing down a hill. "I needed people's help when they sold me, but no one came to my rescue. I can't depend on other people to help me when I need them."

He stopped in the street and turned her to face him. "It must be painful knowing no one rescued you. You must be so angry at people. At God. You must hate all of us, and I can't blame you. We did you wrong."

His words opened a floodgate, and tears streamed down

her cheeks. She hung her head and tried to hide her weakness from him, hide the rage that consumed her.

"I'm sorry, Hannah. People were blinded by the charm of your stepfather, by the hold the madam and the sheriff had on the town. I can't explain why God didn't send someone to your rescue. Sometimes I don't know his will. I don't understand why bad things happen, but I'm here, Hannah. And I know without a shadow of a doubt that God loves all of us. If he can love a sinner like me, I know he loves you as well."

She shook her head. "No. No. No. God deserted me in my darkest hour. I don't think he's out there. I know you believe, preacher man, but I don't."

Wiping her tears, she hurried down the street without him. She had to get away. She couldn't continue staying with Jackson. He made her feel things she never wanted to feel, and she couldn't accept his belief about God.

She just couldn't. No longer would she play the victim for any man. Not even Jackson.

Chapter Nine

Jackson watched as Hannah strode with determined steps down the street toward his home. He'd learned long ago not to push someone too fast. It was best that he give her some time to think about the things they'd discussed. In the meantime, he feared that after this morning's meeting with the sheriff, things could escalate very quickly.

And if the sheriff's vigilante justice came, they'd want to silence Jackson and Hannah. Scare the people then normal lawless life in Hide Town could resume. But what could Jackson do to protect them, besides ride out of town?

A letter to the Texas Rangers was way too slow, unless he sent a rider.

He followed Hannah at a more unhurried pace, giving the woman time to calm down. When he stepped up on the porch of his little house, he heard women's voices. A shiver of alarm trickled down his spine. And he knew…the women from church.

Opening the door, he saw Margaret, Sarah Wright, and Beatrice Smith, but Hannah was nowhere in sight. These women were the nosiest busybodies in his congregation, and he knew what this unplanned visit meant. They were checking on him and making certain Margaret was doing her job as chaperone.

"Ladies," he said, strolling into the house. "To what do we owe the pleasure of your visit?"

Oh, he knew with confidence they were confirming that Hannah was sleeping in her room and Margaret was keeping a close eye on the two of them. They wanted to make certain there was no hanky-panky going on in the preacher's house.

"Reverend, we just wanted to be assured you were settled in, and you have everything you need," Sarah said with a grin like she was offering him her daughter on a platter. He was surprised the young lady wasn't here today.

"I brought you a pie," Beatrice said, smiling at him. "I thought you might be hungry after your terrible ordeal."

Sarah leaned in close, her voice low. "Reverend, we're worried about that woman staying here in the house with you. She's putting you in danger."

"She saved my life. I owe everything to her," he said, not bothering to lower his voice, wanting Hannah to hear he was defending her, standing up to these meddlers. "Margaret is here, and with the women in the congregations help, we're going to show Hannah how good Christian women can help her."

Let them think about that for a moment. Sometimes it was necessary to lead people kicking and screaming by their nose in order for them to realize they were being unjust.

Margaret smiled at the women. "In fact, ladies, I'm hosting a tea for everyone to get to know Hannah. Can you attend tomorrow at three?"

"Margaret," Beatrice said in a disapproving tone. "She's a whore. You don't expect us to mingle with her?"

"Oh, ladies," Jackson said. "Don't you remember the story in the Bible of the woman at the well? The one where Jesus said you who have not sinned throw the first stone? Welcome to the well."

"Yes, but, Reverend," Sarah objected. "Good women do not associate with her kind."

The memory of him turning Hannah away when she'd asked for his help slapped him hard as he now recognized the desperation that had shone from her beautiful emerald eyes. Like so many others, he should have assisted her when she'd asked him.

"And maybe if good women like yourselves would have helped her when she was sold into slavery, then she wouldn't have been thrust into that life. You knew her mother."

"But…she's unclean," Beatrice whispered, shuddering.

"I shared the bed with her last night," Margaret said. "She didn't smell."

Both women gasped.

"In fact, she took a bath early this morning while Jackson was gone," Margaret said.

The image of Hannah, naked and dripping wet, almost had Jackson choking. He swallowed hard and pushed the thought away, wondering where Hannah was hiding.

The two ladies stared at Margaret like she'd lost her mind. "I just don't think I can come to the tea," Beatrice said. "I have small children at home, and I don't want them associating with her type."

"Yet, you're okay living here in town with a vigilante sheriff and a madam who owns most of the town." Jackson stopped and gazed at Beatrice. "Oh wait, I remember your husband's brother Rodney Smith is wanted by the law. That's why you live here. Well, I'm sure he's a fine influence on your children."

Jackson knew he was treading on dangerous ground, but right now, he just couldn't seem to stop himself. The woman was being ridiculous not to accept Hannah, but to think her brother-in-law was all right. Couldn't she see how outlandish her statement was.

Beatrice's eyes widened, and she picked up her reticule. "Sarah, I need to be getting home."

Shaking her head, Sarah sighed and glanced between Margaret and Jackson. "You know, Reverend, I always thought my daughter Priscilla would have been a good match for you, but I don't want her in a house where a soiled dove lives."

There was never any chance he would have considered the young woman. Though the girl was pretty, her personality would never have been conducive to actually caring and looking after the people in his church. His wife would have to be strong yet compassionate.

"Priscilla is a lovely young woman, but if she can't accept me helping people whose lives have been less fortunate, then she would never have made a good preacher's wife," Jackson said, knowing he'd never been attracted to Priscilla, not like Hannah.

The thought stunned him for a moment.

What would a normal everyday life be like with Hannah? One where they weren't chasing or running after bad men? One with children and family surrounding them? The thought surprised him.

"Ladies, I'm going to invite you to tea, and I hope you'll attend, but come with an open heart ready to accept and get to know Hannah. She needs our love and support as she tries to overcome the past. She had to decide whether or not she wanted to live. It's a choice I hope your daughters never have to face," Margaret said with a smile.

She opened the door, clearly telling them it was time to go. The women looked at Jackson then at Margaret as they swept out the portal and hurried down the street.

Margaret dusted her hands off. "And that's what we're up against, Reverend."

With a shrug of his shoulders, he laughed. "They could be more daunting than the sheriff and the madam. But we're going to win this war or die trying."

~

Later that evening, Hannah sat reading a book he'd never seen on his shelves before. He sank down on the sofa beside her and opened his book where he'd left off when his world had been normal, not the crazy life he was currently living.

She glanced over at him. "You're reading."

"Yes," he said and continued on like she hadn't interrupted him.

"It's not the Bible," she said, narrowing her eyes.

"No," he responded, knowing she was intrigued. "I read that every morning to begin the day."

"Oh," she said, going back to her book.

Every little bit, she would glance over at him, trying to see the title. Finally, she sighed. "What are you reading?"

"*The Adventures of Tom Sawyer* by some guy named Mark Twain," he said. "It's really good."

"I've never heard of it," she said and stared at him a few more minutes. "My daddy was one of the smartest men I ever knew, but he didn't read books."

He smiled at her, noticing her blondish-red hair was pulled back away from her face, leaving her looking open and vulnerable. "I've loved books since I was a kid. Lately, I've also been reading these new dime novels by I.M. Lyon."

She glanced at the book he held in his hand. "You're unlike most men."

From the time he was a young boy, life had changed him, shaped him differently from most men, and he was glad.

Drawing his brows together, he acted shocked. "Who me? Just because I like a sense of harmony, not hatred, and don't go around killing people? That's unusual for a man?"

She shook her head. "You know what I mean."

"I don't like to feel pain. And when I see someone else hurting, I feel empathy. Some people would think I'm a sissy, but I'm not." He'd seen enough carnage and men wounded in the war to know bloodshed was not the answer. Even here in Hide Town, people getting killed or injured would not alter the status quo. The attitudes of the townsfolk could only bring about change. But first, Hannah and Jackson had to help them realize life could be different in this renegade town.

Hannah smiled. "You're not a sissy. You saved Melissa. You took a beating."

"I don't believe in killing or hurting or maiming people. But if my back is against the wall, I will do whatever it takes to protect the people I care about," he said softly, wanting her to understand he would take care of her. He knew Hannah was strong and resilient, but beneath that hardened exterior was a soft woman lurking, who was vulnerable to pain. That woman, he wanted to protect and heal.

Licking her lips, she stared at him like she was trying to understand him. "Do you think anyone likes to kill or wound people?"

"Yes, I do," he said, remembering what he'd seen in war. The remembered smells of the dead and injured overwhelmed him, and suddenly, he was thrust back into that nightmare.

Fear rose up inside him, gripping him, holding him hostage. The blood, the mangled limbs of the injured, and a little boy thrust into the horrors of a war he hadn't really understood. The screams of men in unbearable pain still haunted him at night.

Bile rose in his throat, almost choking him with the memories. He blinked rapidly and swallowed hard, pushing the emotions back, but it seemed once the gate was opened, the recollections seemed to flood his mind.

Grown men had gone around stabbing battle survivors with their bayonets, their eyes filled with hate, filled with rage. The sight had sickened Jackson. Killing someone who was just lingering in pain seemed somewhat merciful; whereas, finishing off the men who had a chance at living was sadistic, yet glorious to many soldiers. Maybe Jackson didn't understand or maybe he'd been too young. At the age of ten, war was something that had sounded grand, until he got into battle.

Glancing over at Hannah, he wanted to grab her and hold on, scared of being sucked back into the past.

Her brows drew together in a frown. "Are you all right?"

Forcing a fixed smile on his lips, he sighed. "I'm fine. Probably indigestion from that great dinner Margaret fixed tonight."

"It was good." She gazed at him, her eyes wide filled with concern. "I heard you today talking to those women," she said softly. "Thank you."

"For what? Telling them, they weren't good Christian women?"

Her full lips turned up in a mischievous grin. "No, for standing up for me. It made me feel nice."

Warmth spread through him like the rays of the sun on a cold winter day. She'd heard him talking to the catty women, defending her, trying to help them realize she was just like them, except for the terrible ordeal she'd endured. He knew it would take time, but he wanted Hannah to be accepted into his flock, no questions asked. "Everything I said was true. You deserve happiness just like everyone else."

She closed her eyes.

He reached across the sofa and took her hand. Soft, warm, and delicate, he brought it to his mouth and kissed the center of her palm, letting his tongue glide over her skin, sending a delicious shiver through him. She tasted of lilacs and honey.

He lifted his eyes and gazed into her green ones. "Margaret thinks I should court you."

Part of him was curious to see her reaction. Did she realize this sexual cat and mouse game they were playing was dangerous and rift with emotions that could harm one or both of them? Did she have any feelings toward him or were they just working on a common cause?

She jerked her hand back. "What?"

"Margaret wants me to ask you to marry me."

Hannah's eyes filled with sadness. "I'm hardly what you need. You heard those women. I'm sure many in your congregation feel the same."

"But what about you, Hannah? How do you feel about me?"

"That's not a fair question to ask. You're the first man who's been nice to me in a long time. I care about you, but I'm not the woman who would be best for you."

Jackson felt torn as well. He didn't know what kind of woman he needed. But he did recognize he was enchanted by and even thought he could be falling in love with Hannah. Was he only attracted to her because she needed his help?

Stretching his hand across the sofa, he found hers once again. "You know what I tell the young couples who come to me and want me to marry them?"

"No," she said, watching as he pulled her hand back across the fabric.

"I tell them not to let anyone or anything come between the two of them. Not family, children, work, or distance. Once they are joined together as husband and wife as one, always live with the thought of your loved one's happiness."

He could see tears forming in the corners of her eyes.

"Margaret is sweet to me, but I'm hardly the type of woman who would be the kind of helper you require. Plus…" she said softly, "all the other men."

Maybe he was crazy, but she'd had no choice. The other men didn't bother him. "If someone loves you, that won't matter."

"But it matters to me," she said.

"Hannah, if a man loves you, that won't matter," he repeated. "He will love you for the kind soul you have. He will love you because he needs you to make his life complete."

"I don't think that's possible for me," she said.

Maybe she wasn't quite ready to hear she could have a decent life once this was over, but he hoped in time she would realize she deserved a second chance.

He shrugged. "Whoever I marry, we will be as one. Nothing and *no one* will come between us. I won't let it."

"You've got high expectations, Jackson. And tell Margaret I'm not the girl for you. You saw how those women reacted. Priscilla would be the perfect woman for you."

Throwing back his head, he laughed at the thought of that beautiful mousy girl. He wanted a woman—a lady who knew life was hard and was not ensconced in a dream world.

"Why? Because she's a wimpy version of her mother? Oh no. Whoever I marry should be strong as they're going to have to put up with a lot from the women in whatever congregation I have. The reason I've never married is I've never fallen in love with anyone I thought could handle the constant criticism, pouting, and whining of the other church ladies."

Hannah turned her body toward him and stared, while he continued holding her hand. "Why do you do this? Why did you become a preacher?"

He sighed and thought back to how lost he'd been. How from the time he'd returned from the Civil War at the young age of eleven, he'd been known as a coward. Growing up he'd had to fight his way from one scrape to the next to prove his manhood. Those days had been long and hard, and one day he'd almost killed a man in a fight.

An old man had led him to the church and told him to

put his emotions to good use. He'd fallen in love with the Word and never looked back. "Let's just say God's Word led me out of the darkness."

She laughed. "Well, His Word certainly forgot to give me a candle to show me the way."

He chuckled at her comment. "What was your life like before Elliott married your mother?" He wondered if she'd ever known happy times.

She'd mentioned her father, but what about her mother? The woman had made a terrible choice in marrying Elliott, but what about prior to her second marriage?

Hannah squeezed his hand. "I have only good memories of the days before my father died. We were a happy family, and I never would have believed you if you'd said this would happen to us. Never in a million years would I have imagined my papa dying and my mother remarrying. My parents used to chase each other around the dining room table, and my mother always let my father catch her. They were happy."

Her childhood had been happier than his, and he was glad. How wonderful to grow up with pleasant recollections of your family. He had very few memories of his entire family together. They'd all died when he was young.

She glanced out the window, and he watched as she swallowed hard. "But then Papa was thrown from a wild horse he was trying to break, and he broke his neck. He died before Mother and I found him. I would shoot that animal if I saw him again."

Ranching was dangerous work that often killed men in their prime. Jackson thought about his own father who'd left for the Civil War and never returned. He'd been seven at the time. Three years later, Jackson had joined all the boys heading off to war, not understanding the futility of what they were doing. It'd been the South's last attempt at winning.

"What about you?" she asked. "What about your family?"

"My father and brothers were all killed in the war, and my mother wasted away. She'd lost everyone but me. I'm the only survivor."

And that had come at a cost to his soul, to know everyone in his family had died for a way of life he'd never experienced. No fancy plantation, or fields of cotton, or hundreds of slaves. How could a man approve and fight for a lifestyle that enslaved human beings and call himself a child of God?

"I'm sorry," she said.

He shrugged. "It's why I want my own family, my own children. And I will not be leaving them to go off to war for the rich man. I want to be around to help my boys learn and grow to be great young men."

"What if you have daughters?"

The thought of a family of his own with little ones, both boys and girls, was so appealing his heart swelled at the thought. It had been so many years since he'd had a family. Right now, he had no one but his church. And it wasn't the same.

"Then I'll be here to protect them and watch them grow into beautiful young women with an overprotective father," he said, gazing at her full lips, thinking he would love to taste them again.

Gently, he skimmed his thumb across the top of her hand, and she turned her emerald eyes on his caress.

"Someday, you'll make a great father and husband."

He nodded. "I want to." When he found the right woman, he would honor and cherish her all the days of their life together. Even in bad times, she would be the one he turned to. Maybe it was just a dream, but he hoped not. He'd already lost so much; he wanted a family of his own.

"Your wife will be very lucky," she said, her voice sounding breathy.

With a tug, he pulled her over to his side of the couch, unable to resist her any longer. His hands gripped her head, and he stared into her eyes. "I don't know what it is about you, but you make me want to forget all my vows to remain celibate and carry you off to the bedroom and make love to you. I want to take my time ravishing your body, showing you how it can be between two people who care about each other." He sighed. "But I won't. But by golly, I *will* kiss you."

He lowered his mouth to hers and moved his lips over hers, giving up on any intention of resisting her full mouth. He wanted to consume her, become lost in the tension he could feel swirling around them. He wanted to soothe her pains and banish her memories of the past. He wanted her to know how good it could be between a woman and a man.

Gripping her face, he slanted his mouth for a deeper exploration. One hand tangled in the mass of curls at the back of her head, he brought her closer.

Slowly, her arms wrapped around his back, holding onto him like she wouldn't let go. A thrill of satisfaction gripped his stomach. She'd never done that before, and he knew they'd made progress.

Pressing against her, he felt her breasts crushed against his chest, and it was all he could do not to pick her up and carry her into his bedroom.

She was a temptation he had to indulge in.

The sound of a door slamming had them jumping apart. Quickly, she scooted back across the sofa just as Margaret walked into the room.

Like a naughty schoolboy, he laid his book across his lap to hide the erection standing up in his pants like a flag waving in the breeze.

Margaret glanced between the two of them, and Jackson was certain she had to know they'd been kissing. Hannah's lips were swollen, her breathing heavy, and her curls disheveled.

Clearing his throat, he said, "Did you have a nice visit?"

She gave him a knowing grin that made him nervous. "I had a lovely time. I can see you guys are getting along nicely."

Hannah raised her brows. "We were discussing what books we enjoy reading."

Before Jackson could catch the book, it slipped off his lap and onto the floor.

Glancing at his lap, Margaret shook her head then reached down and picked up the book from the floor. She read the title out loud and glanced down at his lap again then back up into his eyes. "My husband used to take a walk to clear his mind when difficult matters came up. Might I suggest you do the same, Reverend?"

Jackson had to bite his lip to keep from laughing out loud. Instead, he jumped up, actually welcoming the escape. "Great suggestion, Margaret. Good night, ladies."

Chapter Ten

The next morning, Hannah left Jackson's home determined to walk through town and let the people see she wasn't afraid. Plus, she wanted to make certain Elliott's wanted poster was still hanging on the wall outside the sheriff's office for all to see.

Jackson had left the house early this morning, and Margaret had been busy preparing a special dinner for the preacher. Hannah had slipped out, knowing now would be a good time to stroll through town, making her presence known.

As she walked down the wooden sidewalk past the mercantile, the memories of how Ruby had rescued her flooded her mind. Her chest ached with gratitude to the woman she called sister, the person she credited with saving her life. Hannah had been so lost. Her life at such a low point she'd considered suicide. Anything to escape the bordello.

Ordinary people passed her as she walked the short distance to the sheriff's office. The poster still hung on the wall, so she turned away, not wanting another confrontation with the sheriff.

It was then she saw Daniel Gunter, an old client from the bordello. Her stomach clenched as anger rushed through her at the memory of how he'd forced himself on her, beating her for his own satisfaction. He was the worst of humanity, and she knew he was wanted. Dead or alive.

During her training time with Ruby, they'd poured over wanted posters, and when she'd seen his name, she'd hated him even more.

Today was her lucky day. Today, she would earn her first bounty alone. She'd caught wanted men with Ruby's assistance but never by herself.

Determined, she walked toward him. Pulling her gun out of her holster, she took aim and fired, bouncing the bullet in the dirt at his feet.

Dust flew up in a cloud, and he jumped back. His eyes widened when he saw it was her. "What the hell?" His hand moved to his own gun.

Fear exploded inside her, rushing like an avalanche toward her, but just before she was buried beneath the panic, her training kicked in. She took a nice deep breath.

"Please pull your gun. I'd like nothing better than to kill you," she said, her voice low and deadly. "If you want to live, you'll unhook your gun belt nice and slow and sling it far away. If not, I'd be more than delighted to kill you right now."

Of all the men for her to capture for her first bounty, Daniel was someone she would be more than happy to put behind bars. It almost seemed fitting she was arresting him. She reminded herself to breathe nice and slow, calming her nerves, letting her training take over.

"Hannah, I know you've been missing me. We can go right now to Mrs. Hutchins and take care of that itch you have. Hell, we could do it right here in the street, doesn't matter to me."

She knew he was goading her. She knew he wanted her to react to him, but she refused to take the bait. Killing him would be so much easier. There would be no chance for him to escape and hurt someone else. Letting the law hang him would be the best course of action but not the most satisfying.

He moved toward her.

Hannah planted her feet firmly and cocked her gun. "Please keep walking toward me. I promise I will shoot you right here in the street. You're wanted for murder. You're wanted dead or alive. And I aim to collect on that bounty. Now you have a choice, remove your gun belt or give me the pleasure of shooting you. Your choice."

Inside, her nerves were quaking. In her childhood, she'd abhorred violence. As a woman, revenge was her lifeblood.

His brows drew together in a frown. "And you think the sheriff is going to pay you that bounty?"

She shrugged. "Maybe not, but it will give me great satisfaction turning you in. Now you have less than a minute to decide. Do you want to die today?"

She'd never killed a man before. She'd only shot Elliott, but she wasn't backing down. It almost felt like his life or hers, but she'd let him make the decision as to whether or not he wanted to live.

Raising her pistol, she took aim.

"You're serious. You'd shoot me."

"With joy," she said, knowing it wouldn't change what he'd done to her.

He started to unbuckle his gun belt. "After all those nights of pleasure I gave you, you'd shoot me."

She laughed. Why would a man think that hitting a woman gave her enjoyment? He was one twisted soul. "You hurt me physically. I'd love nothing more than to make you feel some of the same pain. But I'm going to do what's right and turn you in to the law."

He slung his gun belt into the street.

"Now start walking toward the sheriff's office."

Smiling smugly, he said. "You know I won't stay in jail long. Sheriff Wyatt is not going to keep me locked up."

"Then you better leave town because the next time I will save the state the time and trouble of giving you a fair trial. I'll just shoot you and collect on the bounty again."

The Sheriff wouldn't be so brazen as to let him go, would he? That could be even more dangerous for Jackson and Margaret.

Daniel started walking toward the sheriff's office, his hands raised in the air. "When I get out, I'm going to—"

"Shut up, Daniel, and keep walking," Jackson said, stepping out of the growing crowd. "Hannah's letting you live. A month ago, she would have just shot you dead."

It was true, Hannah thought with a start. A month ago, she had burned with the need for revenge. Now it was just a warm simmer clenching her gut.

Hannah walked stoically behind the outlaw, keeping her gun trained on him, refusing to look at Jackson. She didn't need his help. She'd been trained as a bounty hunter. She knew what to do next.

As they approached the sheriff's office, she saw he was standing outside waiting on her to reach him. With his hands on his hips, he scowled at her like she was the evil one, not the man who had killed.

"Well, well, Hannah, I see you're stirring up trouble again."

There was more than enough danger already in this town. Hannah didn't have to do anything to stir the problems up. They just naturally occurred.

"No, Sheriff, I'm cleaning up this town. He's wanted for the murder of a sixteen-year-old girl in San Antonio," she said. "There's a wanted poster with his picture on it. I'm sure if you looked at your collection of posters you'd find his name."

The sheriff stared at her like he wished he could kill her right here with all the townspeople watching, but she was no longer afraid of him. Later, when his goons had time to gather their forces, there could be trouble, but now with the good people of Hide Town as witnesses, he wouldn't do anything to her.

"I expect to receive the bounty for turning him in."

"Oh, you'll receive your due soon enough," he said with enough conviction she knew he'd be coming for her.

A trickle of unease wound down her spine like a spider weaving a web. If she were killed, it would just be her time to go, but she couldn't stand the thought of Jackson or Margaret being hurt. They were innocents.

A deputy took Daniel and hauled him inside the jailhouse. The sheriff followed.

As the crowd dispersed, Jackson walked up beside her, his face glowing an unnatural red. "I don't know whether to wring your pretty neck or slap you on the back and say good job. You didn't kill him, which is what you would have done a month ago, but you just stirred up the biggest hornet's nest."

She didn't care. She was prepared for whatever happened, and no other woman would suffer at his hands. "He used to come into the bordello. He's known for beating a woman before he has his way with her. He killed a young girl."

Jackson shook his head. "Come on. Let's get you back to the house. I have some things over at the church I need to get to."

"No, I'm not leaving without my money."

The deputy came out the door and handed her the cash.

"Now, let's go," she said to Jackson.

~

~

Tea was cooling in the pot. The delicate porcelain cups were ready, and a beautiful cake sat beside them on the small table in front of the sofa. Hannah had put on the nicest dress she owned, Margaret was decked out in her Sunday dress…and no one was here.

Ten minutes after the appointed hour and none of the ladies from the church had arrived.

Margaret walked around wringing her hands, and Hannah felt bad for her. She'd gone to so much trouble arranging everything for no one to show.

"I'm sorry, Hannah," she said. "I didn't think it would be so difficult."

Hannah nodded. She hadn't wanted to hurt Margaret's feelings, but after her frigid reception at the small church, she didn't really think the women would want to appear for a social call. "I think you should pour up that tea, and the two of us can have our own little party."

"You're right. Their loss." Margaret sat next to Hannah on the sofa. "It's just I was hoping they would come and get to know you like I have. It's not right. You didn't choose that profession. This could happen to any of their daughters."

And that's what Hannah and Jackson were trying to stop, more kidnappings, more women being forced into a life they didn't want.

"But we're going to pray it doesn't," Hannah said. "I'm hoping what Jackson and I have set in motion will clean up this town. The Texas Rangers should be here any day now and even the Calvary," she said, hoping it was true because if it wasn't, they could be in real danger.

"What about the madam?"

"She's been awfully quiet," Hannah said. "I'm getting worried."

Since the day Hannah and Jackson had ridden back into town, she'd not seen the woman. Sure, the madam's nights were busy, but if Hannah remembered correctly, the woman worked all the time, making sure the nights ran smoothly.

"I don't trust that woman," Margaret said. "She's a she-witch if ever there was one."

A knock sounded on the door, and Margaret's eyes widened. She jumped up and ran to throw open the door.

Two little old gray-haired ladies stood on the front step with their reticules and a covered dish. "Sorry we're late, Margaret, but we had a pie in the oven and wanted to bring it to the reverend. That young man needs fattening up, so we thought one of our buttermilk pies would put some fat on him."

Hannah had suffered disappointment for Margaret when no one showed up, but she'd also felt relief there wouldn't be an hour of small talk from ladies who didn't like her. Now, these two women had arrived.

"Come in, ladies. We're glad you're here," Margaret said.

Hannah rose and stood off to the side as the women entered.

Once they stepped into the house, they turned to stare at her.

"Lucille, I told you she was a beauty," the older woman said. "I'm Clara, and this is Lucille. Nice to meet you."

They didn't offer their hands, just a nod of the head. And Hannah knew they were here to scrutinize her; they weren't really offering her their friendship.

But what did it matter? Her mother had always taught her to be polite to her elders, and she would give these women the respect they were due. But she knew what they were doing. They were inspecting the whore who was living with their reverend.

"Ladies, please have a seat," she said and stepped back to let them choose where they would sit. Every day she felt more certain about moving away from Hide Town and starting over fresh someplace she didn't have horrible memories of and where the townspeople wouldn't label her a whore. Maybe she just needed to move on and put the past in the dust.

Hannah stared at the teapot on the table between her and the elderly ladies sitting on the couch. She didn't dare touch the tea for fear they wouldn't drink it if she served.

Margaret must have realized her predicament because she reached over and poured them each a cup. "We have sugar and cream as well, ladies, if you like your tea sweet."

"You know Sarah and Beatrice are not coming," Lucille said. "They told us Hannah here is sweet on our preacher."

"What?" Hannah said, ready to deny the accusation. Yet, wasn't it true they were sweet on each other? How many times had Jackson kissed her? Did she just think he was doing that to get her on her back?

But they would never be a couple. Women like these ladies would make certain their precious man of God didn't get involved with a woman who'd once been a prostitute.

"Jackson and I are working together to try to clean up the town," Hannah explained.

"So he's not sweet on you?"

Margaret laughed. "Yes, he's sweet on her, but he's trying not to let it show, God love him."

Lucille shook her head. "Girl, you have quite a story, but it's going to make it difficult on Jackson."

Tears welled up in Hannah's eyes, and for a moment, she considered leaving the tea, but then she took a deep breath, raised her chin, and blinked the tears away. "Once we get the town cleaned up to where Jackson can preach without the threat of being beaten, then I'll be leaving. I'd like to get a fresh start where my past can remain in the past."

If she remained a bounty hunter, she wouldn't settle down anywhere, but she didn't know if she wanted to continue with this profession after she'd caught Elliott and cleaned up the town. Sure, she liked wearing a gun, knowing she could protect herself, but chasing criminals didn't seem enjoyable.

Clara's brows rose. "I can understand why you'd feel that way. But if our reverend has chosen you to be the girl to whom he gives his heart, then you'll be his missus, and we'll welcome you as well. Some of the women in our church are just a little tight in their corsets, and it takes them a while to come around. If Jackson chooses you, Lucille and I will make certain you're welcome."

Hannah frowned at the women. So were they accepting her, or was it on condition of Jackson's love? Because if it was, then to hell with them. They could either acknowledge her or not. It wasn't an *if*.

There came a time when Hannah had to defend herself. She'd been victimized enough. She thought of how she could express her feelings.

"Jackson is a wonderful man. He needs a strong wife, but I'm not willing to be allowed into a church only if the reverend marries me. That seems contradictory. I'm still God's creature, and I suffered at the hands of man. If God can forgive me, why can't men and women?"

The elderly women stared at her then glanced at Margaret.

A smile slowly appeared on Lucille's face. She reached out and patted Hannah on the arm. "I think you're going to make an excellent preacher's wife. You're strong enough not to put up with the silliness of some women in the church and support our preacher. Welcome to the congregation."

Hannah frowned. What the hell had just happened? She glanced over at Margaret who was trying hard not to laugh. Were they opening up their arms and receiving her?

"Ladies, he hasn't asked me to marry him, and I don't think I would say yes, even if he did," she said. When she'd left the bordello, she'd never thought of getting married. She was tainted, and no man would ever want her. But then, Jackson had come into her life. He was slowly gaining her trust, and well, she kind of liked the man.

But could he fall in love with her and marry her? So much was uncertain, and she feared more than anything she'd only get her heart broken. She'd suffered enough at the hands of men. She'd never give her heart, unless she was certain her love was returned.

~

Elliott walked into the saloon and looked around. He'd been gone for three weeks, and during that time, the only thing that had changed was that he'd gotten a bullet hole in his arm. Emily was going to be upset with him that he hadn't brought her a new girl, but things hadn't gone as planned.

"Where's Mrs. Hutchins?" he asked the bartender, who was busy restocking the shelves, preparing for the night.

The man turned and glanced at him, raising his brow at the sling Elliott still wore around his arm that was damaged when the bullet ripped a gash from his shoulder to his elbow.

"She's in her office," the bartender answered.

"Thanks." Elliott hurried to the back. When he opened the door, she glanced up.

"Welcome back. Where's my new girl?"

A sigh escaped him. "That damn preacher and my stepdaughter rescued her. Plus, I took a bullet for my efforts."

The madam frowned. "Maybe it's for the best. Those two are stirring up all kinds of trouble here in town. How's the arm feeling?"

"It's better. Still sore as the dickens, but at least I can ride. I honestly think she wanted to kill me."

Emily shook her head. "Elliott, she knows the truth. She knows you didn't owe me money and just sold her to me. You could be in danger."

Fear spiraled through him, gripping his insides like moss, sending blood coursing through his veins. The girl scared him, but he'd never admit that fact to anyone. And for Emily to warn him, she must be concerned too.

He laughed. "From that mousy spit of a girl? I'm surprised the sheriff hasn't put her back to work in your brothel."

"He tried, but she's being protected by that preacher. Together, the two of them have the town all riled up."

Shaking his head, he stared into the cold eyes of the woman he hoped to partner with for a long time. They were good together, but did she realize how much she could do for him? How she could restore his life to the luxury he'd once held until his family had seen it as their job to send him packing? "That girl has learned how to shoot. She could always ride a horse, but I've never seen her fire a pistol so accurately."

The madam smiled an evil grin that made Elliott shiver. "She's telling everyone in town she's a bounty hunter."

A chill washed over him. That spineless twit had caused him nothing but trouble.

"In fact," the madam said laughing. "She's hung a wanted poster right outside the sheriff's office with your face on it."

He cursed beneath his breath. That was exactly what he didn't need. It wasn't the sheriff he was afraid of or even that stupid twit, but some other reckless outlaw who thought he would make a quick bundle on bringing in Elliot.

"If you don't want to swing from a rope, Elliott, I think you need to take care of your stepdaughter."

He frowned. "She's going to ruin everything. I'm going to have to kill her. "

"No, let's try kidnapping her, but if that doesn't work, I think I know how you can catch her," the woman said smugly. "Some things a woman can see on the face of another woman very easily."

"What?"

"That preacher. Get the man, get the girl."

Chapter Eleven

Hannah and Margaret had long ago given up on Jackson coming in for supper. Concern that something had happened to him filled Hannah, but he'd told them he would be late returning.

He'd gone to visit one of the members of his church who had an ailing wife. They lived outside of town and still Hannah worried. She should have gone with him. She could have waited while he'd visited with the family. But no, she'd stayed here, hoping to locate Elliott.

Rumors were floating around town that he was back, and she so desperately wanted to catch him and confront him about the death of her mother. Instead, she waited, while itching to get this fight over with.

"Hannah, I'm going over to Essie Jones' house tomorrow. I think you should go with me."

Turning toward the widow, Hannah searched for a polite way to tell her no. After the disastrous tea, she realized she had no place in this small town. Once this was over, she was moving on.

Being accepted by the two women had done more to scare her than make her feel like she was welcome. She couldn't think about marrying Jackson and being a preacher's wife. That wasn't possible for a woman like her. She couldn't let them convince her she would be welcome. And if she began to believe in the possibility, it would be a crushing blow when she was rejected. As soon as her business here was completed, she needed to leave town forever.

An ache grew in her chest at the thought of never seeing Jackson again, and that shocked her. She'd never expected to have feelings for any man ever again, yet at the thought of Jackson, her body warmed like she'd been out in the sun too long.

There was no future here for her. The best thing she could do would be to continue her life as a bounty hunter, moving on from town to town, never setting down roots. Yet that sounded like such a lonely life. A life she'd never pictured for herself. Not that she'd ever imagined being a whore.

"We just have to keep trying with these ladies. They can be a stubborn group, but they really do have big hearts. And once they welcome you into their homes, they're quite lovely."

Oh no, she wasn't going to expose herself to another of Margaret's schemes to ingratiate her into Jackson's church. She'd had quite enough. She'd opened her mouth to tell Margaret not no, but hell no, when the back door was suddenly kicked in.

There was no warning, nothing, just a boot shoving the door open, sending it crashing against the wall. Two big burly men came rushing in. She yanked her firearm out of its holder, and the man slapped her across the face, knocking her to the ground, sending her gun flying.

The sting stunned her for just a moment as she lay there, while the world tilted crazily.

"Get up," he screamed, pointing his weapon at her. He could so easily kill her, and she knew she wouldn't go down without a fight.

She sprang from the floor, throwing herself into the arms of the gunman, knocking him to the ground. Reaching for his weapon, he rolled her, pinning her to the floor. While his arms held her down, she kicked him between the legs, and he collapsed on top of her, groaning.

The other man attempted to grab Margaret, but she took off running through the house, shrieking like the devil himself was chasing her. A chill surged up Hannah's spine as she watched the woman run toward the place where Hannah knew there was a gun hidden.

The man caught her by snatching Margaret's gray hair, and she squealed even louder, the sound blood curdling, sending fear racing through Hannah, reminding her that the older woman was a lot more fragile than she let on. It was more than Hannah could stand. Another person could not hurt because of her, especially not Margaret, who had accepted Hannah almost from the first, who'd protected her, and tried to help her fit into Jackson's life.

"Stop," Hannah called. "Leave Margaret alone and I'll go with you."

"No," Margaret yelled at the top of her lungs, and the man backhanded the widow.

Hannah screamed, "Stop! If you hurt her, there's going to be a fight."

Jackson sprung through the door, pulling the man off Hannah. Slowly, she rose from the floor.

Jackson pointed his gun on the man who held Margaret, while holding onto the outlaw by his arm. "Let her go," he demanded.

She could see the goon's indecision, but then he looked at the pistol in Jackson's hand as men from the church filed through the door, weapons drawn. Slowly, the intruder dropped his pistol to the floor and raised his hands.

Margaret turned around and yanked the hair on his head.

"Ouch!" he cried.

And she smacked him in the face. "How does that feel? Serves you right for pulling my hair. Didn't your mother ever teach you that's not polite. Only bullies hit women."

Staring at Jackson, Hannah longed to throw her arms around him, but she held back. There were men from his church in the room and hadn't she decided they had no future? But why did the sanctity of his arms look so inviting? Why did she want to rest her head on his chest?

Hannah walked to the older woman's side while Jackson tied up the two men. "Are you all right?"

"I'm fine, dear. A little rattled, but certainly none the worse for the rough and tumble."

As Jackson approached them, he reached out and touched Hannah's cheek. She jumped, surprised at the tender touch of his fingers on the bruise she could feel forming. His fingers were gentle, and she stared into the warmth of his gaze. She'd forgotten how the intruder's punch had struck her cheek.

"You're going to have a bruise," Jackson said softly.

A man came up them. "What should we do with these two?"

Jackson's eyes were gazing into hers, and she could tell he didn't want them to be intruded upon, but they had no choice. She could see the way he watched her wistfully.

Reluctantly, he turned toward the man. "Let's take these two to the sheriff. He should put them in the calaboose."

"I'm going with you," Hannah said, staring at Jackson, knowing she needed to get out of the small house and breath some fresh air. She needed time to think about what had just happened and if she was endangering the people around her.

"No, stay here with Margaret," he said.

"No," she said, refusing. "I'm going with you. I need to get out of here for just a little while."

"Okay," Jackson said, staring at her. "Are you all right?"

She nodded. "Just shaken. Besides, I want to see these two put in jail."

"Well, someone has to stay here since the door is now barely hanging from its hinges," Margaret said.

"I don't think they'll bother us again tonight, but I'm going to have one of the men from church stay with you," Jackson replied.

"You two be careful and make sure those bullies stay in jail. We don't need any more trouble tonight," Margaret said.

Jackson and another man tugged on the ropes and hurried the men out the door with Hannah following closely behind.

What a way to end the night…another confrontation with Hide Town's sheriff.

~

All Jackson could think about was what if he'd been five minutes later. What would have happened? Clearly, they wanted Hannah, but would they have killed her or returned her to the brothel?

His heart beat fast at the thought of them injuring the woman who'd already been through so much. No woman had ever made him want to watch over her, protect her, keep her safe. She deserved so much more than her past. He'd already failed her once; he wouldn't let it happen again.

Her soul was gentle, she was kind, and any woman who could get in Margaret's good graces was first-class. And he liked her. He liked Hannah a lot. So much he was beginning to feel nervous about the idea of her leaving town. After this was over, he didn't want her to go.

Touching her on the arm, he guided her up the stairs to the sheriff's office. One of Jackson's helpers from church pushed the two goons into the office.

"What's this?" the sheriff asked, staring at the group of them, leaning back in his chair.

"I'm filing charges against these men for breaking into my home and assault and battery."

"You boys do that?" the sheriff asked.

They both glanced down at their feet. They weren't exactly boys. They were young men who Jackson suspected of working for the madam.

"We were taking care of business."

"What kind of business?" Jackson asked.

This felt like a set-up. Only two people in this town wanted him and Hannah gone, and one was sitting right here in this room. Would they talk openly in front of the sheriff?

The boy nodded toward Hannah. "We wanted a piece of that girl. After all, she was selling it over at the brothel a couple of months ago. We thought we'd get our share for free."

Rage all but blinded Jackson, and he clenched his fists to keep from smashing them into the boys' faces as he watched Hannah recoil like she'd been slapped.

Then she shook her head as she walked up to them. "That's the most bull-hockey I've heard since I returned to town. You work for the madam. You thought to take me back to where you think I belong. Well, what about your sisters? How would you feel if Elliott stole your sisters and sold them to the madam?"

Jackson almost choked. While she wasn't physically hurting them, she was putting fear into their hearts, letting them know what happened to young women in Hide Town.

The younger of the two men's faces blanched, and he swallowed hard.

"What kind of whore do you think your sister would make?" she said softly, gazing into each one of their eyes. "Should I tell Elliott how pretty they are? A young virgin could make the madam and Elliott a lot of money."

Both young men had large families with younger sisters. Hannah must have known them. Hell, she'd probably gone to school with them.

"Sheriff, let us go," the younger man said.

"Oh no," Hannah said. "Jackson and I are pressing charges. You're going to be locked in here where you can't help your family, and I'm going to whisper their names to Elliott."

The older one hadn't said a word, but suddenly he exploded. "You're a crazy bitch."

Jackson watched in fascination at how she was using her knowledge against the men. He knew she would never do what she was saying. In fact, she was trying to stop Elliott and wanted to see him hanged. But still, the realization of the fear of what *if* it had been their sisters was interesting, if not painful, to watch.

"You keep Elliott away from my family. I'll kill that man if he touches my sister. You understand."

Hannah smiled at the two men. "No, I won't stop him from getting to your sisters. Why should I? You attacked me. Unless you tell me who sent you after me. Then I'll do whatever it takes to make certain they remain safe."

Jackson stepped back and let her talk. He knew, regardless of what these men told them, Hannah would never let any other woman be forced into the bordello, but these boys didn't know that about her. They didn't know she was trying to stop her stepfather and the madam. No telling what the madam had told them to bring Hannah back.

"Now men, I'm not sure Elliott has even returned to town," the sheriff said, his dark eyes worried.

The younger man glanced between the sheriff and Hannah. "Sheriff, you've got to stop him."

Jackson watched her play the men, hoping they'd confess who'd sent them because they both knew it was probably the madam or the sheriff.

Hannah leaned up against the sheriff's desk, crossed one ankle over the other, looked at the men, and sighed. "I'm sure Elliott is starting to get desperate. He lost me, Melissa, and Beth, so I feel certain they need another girl."

"All right. The madam hired us to bring you back," the youngest confessed.

"All you had to do was keep your mouth shut," the older goon said. "Now, we're not going to get paid."

"I don't care. Nobody hurts my family, especially my sister."

The sheriff stood and moved to put them in the cell. "You boys are going to spend some time in here. Think about your loose lips."

"Thank you. Now I can file charges against the madam. Do you hear me, Sheriff?"

"I do. But can you prove it?" he asked. "This boy's word is useless. He's a known drunk, and I'll need more than his testimony to file charges."

"Hey, I'm not a drunk," the young man said, defending his honor.

"I've arrested him more than once for being drunk and disorderly," the sheriff said matter-of-factly.

"You have not," the boy cried.

Jackson shook his head, cringing inside. It was so clear what was happening. But what could he do?

Hannah clenched her fists and raised one at the sheriff. "It doesn't matter. I'm going to get the madam soon. You can tell her I said so."

"Now, don't be making threats against her, or I'll be putting *you* in jail."

"Wouldn't you like that," Hannah retorted.

Jackson was getting that tingly feeling of warning in his spine. He had to get her out of here before the sheriff trumped up charges against Hannah and put her behind bars.

He touched Hannah's elbow, thinking it was time to go.

Suddenly, Hannah straightened and glared at the sheriff. "Where's my bounty? I don't see Daniel Gunter. He's not in the jail."

The sheriff turned and smiled at her. "Oh, didn't you hear? He escaped this morning. We haven't seen him."

As she shook her head, Jackson knew she was just about ready to go off on the sheriff. He stepped up beside her. She didn't seem to realize she was in danger of landing in jail if she opened her mouth and started in on the lawman. Jackson had to protect her.

"Of all the lousy things you've done—"

"Let's go, Hannah," Jackson interrupted her. Then he grabbed her arm and dragged her to the door.

"You're not going to get away with this. You're not."

The sheriff stood back and smiled at her, while Jackson was doing everything he could to get her outside.

Finally, when they were on the wooden sidewalk, she pulled away from him. "Let go of me."

The urge to wrap her in his arms and comfort her was strong, but he knew that would only last a moment, and her hurt was much deeper.

"Hannah," he said softly, "let it go. You can't win that battle." He motioned for the other men that were with them to go on back to the house.

She turned on Jackson as they walked down the street. "He let that man go. He did that on purpose."

"And he'll probably let those other two goons go as well," he said.

"This is impossible. We're never going to clean up this town and make it right. They're going to win. I'm going to find myself back in the brothel…"

He wrapped his arms around her, and she leaned her head on his shoulder.

"I'm scared."

"I'm frightened as well," he said, rubbing his hand down her back in a soothing gesture. "But we can do this."

She lifted her head from his chest, and he stared into her emerald eyes, feeling himself falling into a vortex. He covered her mouth with his. Right here, at the corner of Main Street and Church Avenue, he layered his mouth over hers and kissed her like it was his last kiss.

After stepping into the rectory this afternoon and seeing Hannah struggling to fight off the criminals, he'd felt like his world was crumbling. What if they'd hurt her? What if Hannah disappeared?

The thought of them harming her had him holding her tighter. No matter what happened in the coming days, he wanted Hannah to safely get through this, even if he didn't.

He kissed her like he'd never let her go, and he didn't want to let her go. She felt like she belonged right here in his arms. Her breasts were smashed against his chest, and he felt himself hardening against her thigh.

If only they weren't here in the midst of town where anyone could see them. His mind went a thousand different directions on what he'd like to do to her. Things a preacher was taught never to think about. But he couldn't help himself with Hannah. He wanted her, and if they weren't in the middle of Main Street, he would have taken her.

"Good evening, Reverend," a couple called out to him from across the street.

He released Hannah's lips, staring down into her soul, his breathing heavy and rushed. What was this woman doing to him? Why did he forget everything once he found himself in her arms? And how could he imagine living a day without her by his side?

His parishioners!

"Good evening," he called, knowing he'd been spotted, and by morning, his congregation would be up in arms about him kissing Hannah. But he didn't care. All he could think about when he was near her was Hannah. Sweet, delicious, delectable Hannah.

Tilting her head, she stared up at him. "You are a surprise, Reverend. Every time I'm ready to give up, you breathe life back into me."

Shaking his head, he smiled. "In the literal sense, you're right."

Chapter Twelve

The next morning, Hannah slipped out before Margaret had the opportunity to try to wrangle her into attending that silly women's function again. The woman had been good to her, but right now, Hannah's focus must be on locating Elliott, so she could finish her job and get out of Hide Town before her heart was broken once again.

Jackson and she were dancing a dangerous waltz—a waltz where someone was going home hurt. If she wasn't careful, it would bring one or both of them down.

She dropped into the sheriff's office and saw both of their prisoners were still being held. She felt a smidgen of relief, knowing they were still locked behind bars.

Strolling down the street, she stopped in and checked with Tim the stable boy to see if he'd seen Elliott.

Nothing.

The man was laying lower than a rattlesnake in a gravel pit. She knew he would soon turn up, but where and when?

Finally, knowing Margaret would be gone, Hannah hurried back to the house, determined to eat a quick bite and go out searching again. The man had to be somewhere in this town, and she would find him.

She'd just finished eating some leftover ham when she heard a knock outside. Suspicious, she pulled her gun and peeked out the window. Two little ladies from Jackson's congregation stood at the door, dressed prim and proper, their hats shading their faces.

She opened the door. "Hello, ladies," she said. "Jackson is at the church."

"Is Margaret here?" one of them asked.

"No, she's gone to a ladies' tea. I just came back to grab some lunch. Then I'm leaving."

"Could we come in?" the older one asked, pushing past Hannah and stepping inside without an invitation.

Shaking her head, Hannah couldn't help but think that for little church women, they were certainly offensive.

The first woman glanced around the house as if she were looking for evidence that Hannah was sleeping with Jackson.

Hannah stepped aside and opened the door wider. "Come right on in and have a seat. Can I get you anything to drink?"

These women were coming in whether Hannah wanted them or not. That couldn't be good.

"Oh no, we won't be that long. I'm Mabel," the older lady said, sitting down on the sofa.

"Justine." Neither woman offered to shake Hannah's hand.

It suddenly dawned on Hannah how cold they were being toward her, and she realized who their husbands were. A shiver skittered down her spine like a squirrel dancing on a barb wire fence. Both of their husbands had visited the brothel on a regular basis.

Nausea roiled through her stomach like the bow of a ship in a storm. She'd serviced both men. She'd helped them cheat on their wives, and that didn't sit well with her.

"Margaret should be back in the next hour," she said, knowing she didn't want to entertain them long. What could these women want?

"Our business is with you," the older lady said. "We heard some disturbing news this morning and wanted to hear your version."

"What?" Hannah asked, not certain as to what they were referring.

"Someone told us that you and the reverend were seen kissing last night on Main Street. Is this true?"

Now it all made sense. They were here to cause trouble for Jackson and her for kissing out in public. Out in the street, he'd laid one on her pretty heavy last night, but they'd just dealt with a life and death situation, not to mention carting two criminals to justice. And it wasn't like they'd come home and jumped into bed together.

"Yes, the reverend kissed me last night after fighting off two gunmen who were going to kidnap me and harm Margaret," she said unapologetically. She didn't care what they thought of her, but she didn't want to harm Jackson's prominence in the community.

"Dear…your reputation is hurting the reverend. I know you think a lot of him. After all, the man did save your life."

"What? No, I saved his life."

Mabel crossed her legs at her ankles and clasped her gloved hands together. She gave Hannah a frown that clearly showed she didn't believe her. "Sure you did."

Stunned, Hannah stared at the two women. "They had beaten him almost unconscious. I rescued him."

"It doesn't matter, dear," Justine said.

"So what are you here for?" Hannah asked, already counting the moments until they left.

Mabel glanced over at Justine. "We just think it would be in the reverend's best interest if you were to leave town. Quietly disappear, so he does not have to make a choice between the church and you."

Hannah took a deep breath and released it slowly, trying to quell the urge to punch the woman. Of all, the black-hearted things to say. That Jackson would have to leave the church if he continued to kiss her. Sure, she was already planning her departure once this was over, but these women didn't need to know that. And most certainly, she didn't appreciate them telling her to disappear. "What makes you think he would have to choose between his church and me?"

"Dear, it's obvious you've not changed if you're kissing a man on Main Street. The reverend is a nice young man, and we just don't want him to choose to go down a path that resembles Sodom and Gomorrah."

Hannah felt like she'd stepped into a blizzard, her blood freezing in her veins. "Sodom and Gomorrah? What's that?" she asked, pretending ignorance, needing to hear them say the words, what they were comparing her to.

"You know, those hedonistic sexual perverts who God punished."

"Well, we certainly don't want to go down that path, do we," Hannah said, anger building like an avalanche screaming down the mountain to cover these women.

"That's why we think it would be best if you left town and left our reverend alone."

Nodding while her heart wrenched inside her chest, the truth slammed into her. His church would never accept her, and she wondered why she felt so disappointed. She'd known from the beginning they believed she'd chosen this lifestyle, or maybe they didn't care and just saw her as soiled goods. Whatever their reasoning, they didn't want her near their pastor. In fact, they wanted her gone.

No one told Hannah Williams what to do any longer. No one.

"Are you ladies married?" She knew they were. Blinded by their hatred, she could feel the need to respond to their meanness building inside her. This wasn't going to end pretty.

Mabel smiled, a sweet turning up of her lips. "Yes, John and I have been married for close to twenty years."

"What about you, Justine?"

"Frank and I have been together close to twenty years as well and have two kids."

"And your husbands are John Meacham and Frank Clark?"

"Yes," they both said.

Hannah nodded. "Oh, ladies, I remember them." Then, shaking her head, she made a sympathetic tsking noise. "I'm so so sorry."

"What?" Mabel said.

Justine suddenly stood. "Let's go, Mabel." Her hands gripped her reticule like her small bag contained a million dollars. She began to pace the floor.

Hannah released a deep breath, crossed her arms, leaned back against the wall, and casually put one ankle over the other. "They must be such an embarrassment for you two women. If you're worried about Sodom and Gomorrah, are they going to leave town as well?"

Mabel shook her head, looking confused. "Of course not. Why would they need to leave town?"

Hannah smiled at Mabel. "Does John still have that mole just to the right of his pecker? You know the one he calls his star power?"

Mabel's eyes widened, and her mouth dropped open. "How do you…?"

What did she think her husband was doing over at the saloon? Just playing cards and drinking? Hannah knew what she was doing was wrong.

She'd been forced to be a prostitute, but the men hadn't. She was tired of being beaten down, and she just couldn't turn the cheek another time. Enough.

"And Frank…" Hannah laughed. "The girls in the brothel used to call him horsey behind his back because he would sound like a braying mule whenever he had sex."

Justine threw back her shoulders and marched toward the door. "Let's go, Mabel."

"That's not true," Mabel said. "My John would never…"

Good grief, did Hannah have to give her all the details before this woman believed her man was cheating on her?

"What? Purchase a prostitute? Then can you tell me where he was Saturday night until about eleven? I know he loved to drink whiskey, but he also liked to fool around with the girls. He especially liked Clara and only took me when she was busy and he didn't have time to wait."

Justine shouted over her shoulder as she hurried out the door, "Mabel, I will meet you outside."

"No, wait for me. I'm right behind you." As she all but ran out the door, she glanced back over her shoulder and shouted, "You're evil! Filled with the devil."

Hannah couldn't stop herself. "Not anymore."

Mabel almost ran over Justine. She couldn't get away from Hannah quick enough.

Hannah walked to the open doorway and called out, "Ladies, Margaret will be back just any time now. Are you sure you don't want to wait?"

Screaming in horror, the two women hurried down the path to the street, away from the house, with Hannah close on their heels.

Dang it, if they were going to come where she was staying to make her feel bad, she would give them back tenfold.

"Does this mean you won't be inviting me over for tea?" she called from the front step. "I was really wanting to get into the quilting group. Next time give me some notice, and I'll be sure to have cookies baked."

Mabel turned and shook her fist at Hannah one last time. "Harlot. You're the spawn of the devil!"

"Bye, ladies. I enjoyed our chat," she called out before slamming the door.

All the bravado she'd felt buoying her suddenly melted onto the floor like a snowman in July, leaving her an emotional, mad wreck.

She was trying to face her past and trying to no longer be a victim, but it was hard when people couldn't see beyond the woman who'd been forced to work in a brothel. It didn't matter to some people that she'd had no choice. Once a soiled dove, always one. No forgiveness, just live as an outsider not accepted by society, or return to the brothel.

Sitting in the living room with her head in her hand, she thought about what the women had said. She was ruining Jackson's reputation. She was endangering Margaret and Jackson, while eating his food and sleeping in his guest bedroom.

What was she thinking?

She needed to leave now before he came home, before Margaret returned and tried to convince her to stay. She needed to leave before her heart became entangled with Jackson's any further. There was no hope for romance between the preacher man and the soiled dove. No chance at all.

Tears welled up in her eyes, and before she could change her mind, she hurriedly packed her few belongings and left the house.

She didn't belong here. She didn't belong with Jackson. She didn't belong with any man.

~

Jackson loved being a preacher, but dealing with some members of his congregation was like walking barefoot through a cactus patch. Thorny, dangerous, and just painful. When Mabel and Justine had come to the church early this morning to warn him about the sins of Hannah, he'd done his best to be polite and listen to the ravenous women, but they both had eligible daughters they wanted him to court, which blinded them to the scriptures about forgiveness. Though he'd pointed them in that direction and ushered them out the door.

Tonight, he hoped Hannah, Margaret, and he could have a quiet dinner, and afterwards, maybe read a while before they each went to their own beds—where he would lie awake and listen for the sound of Hannah's breathing, hoping she would sneak down the hall to his bed, realizing he was being foolish for even considering that she would want him. The brothel had turned her against love.

He had to show her she deserved happiness just as much as any other woman or man, but she didn't want a man. And could he blame her? The brothel had stripped her of the normal desires between a man and a woman.

Margaret met him at his front door, her gaze worried. "Have you seen Hannah?"

"No, why?" he asked.

"She's not here, and her things are gone," she said, wringing her hands. "I'm worried about that girl. Do you think she's been kidnapped?"

Fear clutched at Jackson's chest and spiraled down his spine like a rattler slithering through the grass. "They wouldn't have let her take her things, if she'd been kidnapped."

"Maybe that madam took her things, so it would look like she went back to that den of sin."

Shaking his head, he glanced across the street and saw the small building where they worshipped. The day had started off with a visit from his snootiest, most backstabbing congregation members, the ladies who stirred up more trouble than a dust storm during a drought. "You attended the luncheon today."

"Yes," Margaret said, exasperated. "Some Christian women need to be reminded about how fortunate they are."

The memory of him kissing Hannah on the street last night had stayed with him all day. He'd enjoyed every minute. But looking back, he realized it would have been better if they hadn't been out in the middle of town, where everyone could observe them.

Jackson smiled at the older woman, knowing last night's kiss would be zipping through town faster than a Pony Express rider. "What was the topic of conversation?"

"At the luncheon, you and Hannah. Some women in that church think there is hanky-panky going on in this house. I set them straight right away that this girl is a sweet woman who's been dealt a bad hand in life. I quoted scripture to them, but I don't know if they heard."

People didn't want to hear the scriptures that reflected their life. They only wanted the ones pointed toward their neighbor.

"Did they mention seeing us kiss last night on Main Street?"

"Yes. I wondered what you were thinking, Jackson. That was hardly the time or the place to show your affections."

Oh, knowing these women, they'd probably made a beeline straight to his house, when they couldn't get his attention this morning.

He ran his hand through his hair. "You're right, Margaret. But sometimes the spirit moves you and that's where it happened. I think I have a good idea of why Hannah left, and I know the only place she'd go."

He grabbed his Stetson from the peg beside the door, where he'd hung it less than five minutes ago and shoved it on his head. "I'm going to fetch her."

Walking out the door, he heard Margaret yell, "Don't you think you should tell me where you're going in case something happens?"

Knowing she was right didn't stop his feet from moving forward. Hannah was in danger, and while he knew she'd argue with him, he wasn't going to let her sneak back

to that little cabin and live there alone. He didn't give two
hoots and a holler what his congregation thought about her
living with him. The woman needed his love and support.
And he got the feeling that today his parishioners had
reached out and given her a shove out the door.

Well, it wouldn't work.

~

Hannah had missed the coziness of the little cabin.
She'd forgotten how this place had been her own little
hideaway up until the night she'd rescued Jackson. That
night seemed so long ago, though it'd only been weeks.
Yet, so much had happened since the day she'd rescued
him from the madam's goons.

At first, she'd hated him for how he'd turned his back
on her. But then, she'd come to realize he'd not understood
the circumstances and actually felt remorse for what he'd
done. Jackson was a kind-hearted man, and she could see
how that probably got him into more trouble than he was
willing to admit.

Still, leaving him was for the best, for his safety and for
Margaret's, and also so his church women would no longer
have to worry about his virtue. They didn't realize Hannah
had no interest in seducing a man. Let alone a man of God.
She didn't want or need anyone in her life.

Now she could focus more on her goal of capturing
Elliott and ruining the madam's business. Once those
things were accomplished, then she'd move on her way and
leave Jackson and Margaret, her friends, behind.

Laying on the bed, she glanced up at the ceiling and
wondered what her life would be like if her mother was
still alive. She was fantasizing about her mother when the
door slammed against the wall.

Jumping straight up, she yanked out her guns. Jackson walked in the door, looking better than a sack of gold. His brows were drawn and a frown graced his face.

"You know, preacher man, I'm about to get tired of men using their feet to enter a building. If you can't knock, then don't bother coming in." She shoved her guns back in their holsters.

"We're back to *preacher man*. For the last few weeks it's been Jackson, but now you've erected that wall again."

She tossed her head back and gave a sarcastic laugh. "The wall never came down. But *preacher man* seemed to get under your skin, so I liked to use it to irritate you."

"Up until I left this morning, you were calling me Jackson. What's changed?"

Shrugging, she turned and walked away, giving him her back. How could she tell him two ladies in his church had convinced her she was a bad influence.

He sat at the small table and glanced up at her. "You know I was looking forward to coming home tonight and sitting around the table, having dinner with you. Then I imagined we'd do a little reading, while you and Margaret could sew your needlework. A nice evening at home after the night we had last night."

The picture he painted with his words, left her chest aching and her longing to return to his home. But she didn't belong there. "You could still have that with Margaret."

"Not the same. I want you there. What happened?"

She would not prattle on about how his church women had encouraged her to leave town. She'd mishandled the situation completely, but at the time, her need to wound them, like she was hurting, had been fulfilled. Probably not her finest ten minutes. "Nothing. I just decided maybe you'd be safer with me out of your home."

He shook his head. "You know, first thing this morning, I had a visit from two of my female parishioners who I love to call my naysayers. You know that tale of Chicken Little, the little chicken that runs around saying the sky is falling and everyone prepares for the worst. That's these two women."

"So? Maybe the sky is about to fall."

For all she knew, death could be imminent. Still, she'd let two women convince her she shouldn't associate with this man. Yet, when she was with him, it felt right. Like this was where she belonged.

"No, I think when they couldn't get through to me, they decided to go visit Jezebel herself. You." He paused, watching her closely. "Did you get a visit from Mabel and Justine?"

She walked over to the counter, where she'd set a clean bowl of water. Taking the dipper, she took a drink then put it down. While he was here, this was not what she wanted to talk about. She yearned for something she'd never thought she'd long for again.

"How did Margaret's luncheon go?" she finally asked, trying to steer him away from the events of today and her reasons for leaving.

"Don't change the subject. Did they visit you?"

Crossing her arms over her body, she stiffened. "Yes, they came to warn me about ruining their beloved preacher. How I must be the spawn of Satan to go after their precious man."

"And did you tell them about their husbands going to the brothel?"

She stared at him in surprise. "How did you know?"

He laughed. "I know you. When your back is against the wall, you come out swinging." Then he shrugged. "Actually, the two couples weren't too happy to see either one of us return to town."

Still, they didn't deserve to learn their husbands were cheating on them from an ex-soiled dove. "I'm sorry. I didn't handle it very well. Both women ran from the house," she said with a sigh. "They're right, Jackson. I'm not good for you. I'm ruining your reputation. I have no right to be close to you. I should live alone."

Grabbing her arm, he pulled her down until she fell into his lap. It was a first for her, to sit on a man's lap with his arms wrapped around her. A sense of rightness overcame her.

"Remember the woman at the well. Those of you who are without sin, throw the first stone. None of us are without sin. Not me, not you, and definitely not my church women."

"I can't stay with you any longer, Jackson," she said in a whisper that was filled with all the pain flooding through her like spring rains. "I just can't."

What could she say to him without letting him know her true feelings? She cared deeply for him, and all she could ever receive for her emotions was heartache.

"Why?" he asked. "You're safe with me."

"No, I'm not," she said. "You're awakening feelings in me that long ago died, and it scares me."

He pulled her mouth to his and plundered her lips. He grabbed her head and held onto her like he was adrift in the sea and she was his anchor. His mouth promised her tomorrow, but her heart failed to believe.

After several moments, he broke apart from her. "I'm more terrified of living without you than I am of exploring this thing between us. I need you, Hannah."

Chapter Thirteen

Overcome with emotions warring against each other, Hannah only knew she needed to be in Jackson's arms. Never before had she wanted a man to hold her, kiss her, and to feel her skin against his, but with Jackson, it wasn't just a need. It was a necessity. She felt she couldn't live another moment without touching his skin, without kissing his lips, or trusting him.

Sure, she was no virgin. She knew what happened between a man and woman, but she'd never before craved or longed to join with a man. In fact, she'd hated the very act. But now, she ached with the need to be with Jackson. And that shocked her.

His mouth ravaged hers as his hands gripped her head, holding her captive, consuming her lips. Her hands raked his back, coming around to his shirt front, where she released the buttons. Slipping her hand inside his shirt, he moaned when she touched his flesh, and she shivered at the feel of his rippled muscles beneath her hands.

Jackson was so strong. If only he could be her man.

"Oh, Hannah, what you do to me," he whispered, his lips barely leaving hers before he wreaked havoc on her mouth again.

No man had ever kissed her like this. His lips were like flames licking her body, scorching her with their heat. His words sent ecstasy shivering through her, increasing her longing like a stampede on the prairie.

Pushing his shirt past his shoulders, she wanted to feel his naked chest, needed to touch his skin with hers. When his arms were trapped by the shirt, she leaned back, breaking the seal of their lips and gazed into his brown eyes.

This man had her believing in people again, believing in him. He saw the goodness when she could only see the dishonorable way individuals treated one another. He'd defended her, accepted her, and now she wanted to share with him the most intimate act on earth. For the first time in her life, she required a man, but not any man…only Jackson.

She craved and yearned for them to join together.

Slowly, she unbuttoned her shirt then pulled the garment over her head and tossed it onto the floor. Her chest rose and fell under her chemise as she stared at him, nervous and hesitant and filled with need for him, into his warm gaze.

"Are you certain, Hannah?"

"Yes," she whispered. "Please show me the beauty of what happens between two people who care for each other. Cleanse me and make me whole."

She wanted to say make love to me, but she'd never been in love before, and she wasn't certain whether what she felt for Jackson was love or gratitude. She had to know for sure before she uttered those words because once she did, they would be forever.

"Oh, my stars," he said. "I can't resist you any longer. I've been hungering for you for weeks."

After lifting her chemise over her head, she sat in his lap with her skirt and pantaloons still on, naked from the waist up. Fear crept along her spine, and she trembled. What if he didn't like her body? What if he thought she was dirty? What if…?

His fingers trailed across her cheekbone, slowly down her neck, her chest. She whimpered, her body tensing with need.

Oh God, how she wanted him to touch her breasts, her nipples, but he traced his fingertips between her breasts to her waist.

Then he glanced up into her eyes and smiled. "You're stunning."

Tensing, she cried out, "Jackson."

No one had ever taken the time to caress her breasts. No man had taken his time with her body. She'd been nothing more than a vessel they'd used for their gratification.

Pushing the thoughts away, she vowed to keep her focus on Jackson, to return the pleasure he was giving her.

Leaning down, he sucked her breast into his mouth, licking her nipple, sending shivers scurrying through her body.

Rubbing her hand through his hair, she moaned deep in her throat. "What are you doing to me?"

"I'm worshipping your body. You're beautiful, Hannah. I want to make you feel special."

She sighed, letting her body relax and enjoying the feel of his mouth against her chest. She skimmed her hands down his naked back and longed to feel the two of them touching, skin against skin.

Standing, she backed away from his lips. Slowly, she unbuckled her belt, unbuttoned her skirt, and slid the garment down her body. His eyes grew larger as she hooked her thumbs into the waistband of her pantaloons and guided them to the floor. Stepping out of them, she turned and faced him naked.

He licked his lips and moaned, the sound more of a growl. Jumping from his chair, he shucked his boots, his pants, and the rest of his clothing. Then he locked the door, picked up her hand, and led her to the bed in the corner of the room.

"Hannah, whatever happened in the past is now the past. Today is a new beginning for you, for us, and for tomorrow."

His lips captured hers, his mouth moving over hers, giving her breath. He held her tightly to him like he'd never let her go. It was a torturous kiss filled with secret desires and dreams of a normal life with Jackson at her side.

Gently, his hands molded her soft curves against his muscular frame, letting her feel every hard ridge of him. The musky scent of him enveloped her, wrapping around her like his arms, filling her with desire. All she wanted was to join with him here. *Now.*

Oh my, how she wanted him to seal the empty places in her soul, to replace the nightmares of old with dreams of the two of them.

Breaking off the kiss, he gripped her hands with his, holding her naked body tight against his own. "Oh, Hannah," he whispered against her neck. "Sweet temptation."

She trembled, his words, thrilling her.

After pulling the rough blanket back, he laid her on the bed and crawled in beside her. For a moment, he held her in his arms, his hands tenderly rubbing her face, his fingers trailing over her lips, down her throat.

"I'm scared," Hannah whispered, gazing into his soft brown eyes.

"Don't be," he said, his voice husky. "You're more than I ever wanted."

"But…what if I can't?"

"We'll go slow."

His lips covered hers, and she knew she wanted to experience it all with Jackson. She didn't want to hold anything back any longer. She'd never wanted a man before tonight, but now she had to have this man. *Her man.*

An overwhelming sense of rightness permeated her, and she relaxed against Jackson. She'd trust this man with her life. She could trust him with her body. Slowly, he stroked her skin, caressing her like she was a cherished piece of china.

This was Jackson, *her* Jackson. The man whom she'd saved, who stood with her to clean up the town and close down the brothel. The man who accepted her regardless of the past and cared for her despite her faults.

Though she'd never imagined experiencing love, she was falling in love with Jackson, her preacher man.

Stroking his manhood, she felt the velvety softness of his hardened shaft and teased the end with her fingertips.

He grabbed her hand, halting her movements. "Tonight is about you. There will be time for me later."

His hands were sliding down her body, stroking every inch, touching her everywhere, and making her feel worshiped and cherished. Searching and finding her very center, he delved his fingers into her hot, moist core.

Amazed at the feelings he evoked, she sighed, a delicious sound filled with longing. Never had she been exposed to the frenzied passion Jackson was stoking. Never had she wanted a man to hurry and place his penis in her. She ached with a desire she'd never experienced before, and need roared within her.

Shivering with a wantonness she'd never felt before, she whimpered, "Jackson."

Rising up, he positioned himself at her entrance.

Panting, she reached down and pushed herself on him—needing him, wanting him like she'd never longed for a man before.

In no way had she enjoyed joining with a man until Jackson. Only this man made her feel like a woman. Her heart felt emotions she'd long since given up on ever knowing. Jackson made her hunger for desire, and at no time had she thought she would understand that emotion.

She craved him, and the pure joy she felt at that thought thrilled her. Kind, brave Jackson had battled for her, protected her and sheltered her. And she wanted to give him her heart in return for what she hoped would be his love.

Like a pirate seeking gold, he ransacked her lips, sweeping her mouth with an incessant hunger that gripped her, holding her captive with his lips. His body filled her, plunging deep within her, giving her pleasure, cleansing her soul.

She welcomed his driving force giving her a sense of homecoming and fulfillment, she'd never felt before.. This was the man she wanted to spend forever with, to grow old and have babies with. This was the man she wanted to love and cherish until the day she drew her last breath. This was the man she'd fallen in love with.

Oh no…

A tightness gripped her body, and lights shattered through her.

"Oh my," she cried out, hanging onto Jackson like a port in a storm.

Shudders rippled through her, leaving a sense of satisfaction. In Jackson's arms, she felt not only security and pleasure, but a growing sense of love. Was this how it felt when you loved someone?

With a cry and a convulsive quake, Jackson slammed his body into hers, driving himself deeper into her womb. Then he rested on top of her, his body shaking, his breathing raspy in her ear.

Together, they lay helpless, sweating, completely undone by what had just happened.

Happiness filled her chest to the point she ached from the love surrounding her. Teardrops welled in her eyes and trickled down her cheeks. The girls in the brothel had talked about orgasms, but Hannah had never understood until today.

Tears streamed down her cheeks. She cried for the girl who'd lost so much and for the woman who'd just discovered love.

~

Jackson rolled them over and cuddled Hannah's warm, soft, delicious body to his. Their time in the cabin was quickly running out, but she needed to feel beautiful and desired, and all he could think about was wishing this night would never end.

She sniffed and he sensed her crying.

"What's wrong?" If he'd hurt her, he didn't think he could live with himself because he'd held back, trying to make certain she was enjoying their lovemaking as much as he. And oh, how he'd tried to make this good for her.

"Nothing," she whimpered.

"Did I hurt you?"

She rolled over to face him, tears running down her cheeks. "No. It's just…"

"What, Hannah? Was it awful? Terrible? Please tell me because I've not been with many women, and I've never had someone cry afterward."

After everything she'd been through, she probably hated having sex with him. He'd been the worst and now she was crying.

"No, it was beautiful. I've never experienced anything like what we just did. I've never reached an or…"

Jackson felt like someone had just set off a box of explosives at a fourth of July picnic. Tenderly, he reached out and wiped away her tears. "I don't like to see you cry. I would never intentionally hurt you. I'm glad what we did tonight was good for you. I feared you would hate being with me."

Protectiveness filled him, and he wanted to shield her and care for her and keep her from harm. She'd suffered so much because of Elliott. All Jackson wanted to do was guard and defend her. Her big emerald eyes filled with tears, and he watched them roll down her cheeks again.

"I feared I would never want to be with any man, but you made it special. You made me feel beautiful and wonderful."

He pulled her tight against him. "I want to be with you."

"You can't be with me. Your church has made it clear they will never accept me."

Jackson refused to believe good Christian people could not forgive the sins Hannah had been forced to commit. He shook his head. "No, Hannah, it won't happen overnight, but people will come to accept you again. And some people will be upset with me. I might even lose a few parishioners. People will come around. God forgives."

The urge to ask Hannah to marry him was strong, but Jackson held off, not wanting their life together to begin in bed. He wanted to propose properly. He wanted to give her what she deserved. A wedding, a home, and a family.

A shiver went through him, and he jerked against her.

Her voice was soft. "Tell me what happened to you, Jackson. Why do you refuse to kill?"

Her words yanked him right out of the nice warm cocoon he'd felt himself slipping into. The memory of his past was painful, and the only time he let it come into his mind was when he was dreaming and had no control. But she deserved to know what had happened. Once they were man and wife, she would have to live with his nightmares.

"When I was ten, the Civil War was in its last days. The South was desperate for soldiers. They would take just about anyone, including boys. My southern family wanted their son to be in the 'Great War.' So they signed me up and shipped me off right after my tenth birthday."

He shuddered at the memory, his chest tightening with the pain of how he'd joined the regiment, marching, carrying a gun, and helping shoot boys, men, anyone who wore the color blue, until…

"It was quite an adjustment to a scholarly schoolboy like myself. Sure, I played war with my friends, but the reality was a hundred times worse than I'd ever imagined. Before the Battle of Sayler's Creek, I ran away. I deserted." His chest ached from the memories of what had sent him bolting like a coward.

"Oh Jackson, you were a boy. A child. How could anyone hold you accountable for running away?"

"I couldn't kill again. I couldn't pull the trigger and end a life. I just wanted to go home."

She rubbed his back. "You were so young."

"There was so much blood everywhere. Men moaning and dying." Jackson shrugged, trying to shake off the memories, which still haunted him. "I told everyone the general sent me home, told me he wanted me to live. But I lied. Three days after that battle, Lee surrendered and most of my platoon was dead."

She lay motionless in his arms. "What about your family? What did they say when you returned home?"

He shook his head. "That was the worst part. They were all dead, even my mother. Died from typhoid. I was lucky. A family took me in and raised me until I went out on my own."

Brushing her hair back, he kissed her neck. She turned in his arms and gazed at him, her eyes shining with a sweetness that filled his soul. How could he ever live without her?

"You're a good man, Jackson Colster. You'd be dead if you hadn't run. Thank you for telling me and thank you for tonight."

Leaning down, he kissed her on the lips, wanting to fill her with joy again, but knowing their time was at an end. Reluctantly, he released her mouth. "We need to get back before Margaret sends a group looking for us."

"I don't think I should go back."

"Then I'm staying here with you. I'll be fired from the church, or Margaret will move in as well," he said. "I'm not leaving you alone."

She reached up and caressed the side of his face with her hand. "I don't want you to be fired. And there's not enough room here for all of us."

"Then I guess we better get back," he said, happy that she would return with him. He didn't want her far from his side for even a little while.

"All right, I'll go back with you." Her brows drew together and she bit her lip. "I hope I don't get you fired for having sex without the bond of marriage."

He smiled, unable to think of what had happened between them as a sin, knowing he would soon make it right. "I've committed worse sins, but this one was well worth every minute spent in your arms."

He hadn't led by example, yet he hoped what he shared with Hannah had been healing to her. And he had every intention of making her his wife as soon as the time was right. In fact, he wanted it sooner rather than later because he didn't know how he'd resist her now he'd laid with her. Oh yes, they needed to get married soon.

She reached up and touched his lips. "We better go. Margaret will be worried."

"Yes," he said, and they both stood and dressed.

He'd found paradise in her arms tonight, and once everything was settled, he had every intention of making her his, permanently.

~

When they returned to the house, Margaret was waiting. She turned and glared at both of them, looking like she'd caught two kids playing hooky from school. "Just where were you, missy?"

"I went back to the cabin I'd stayed in before I rescued Jackson," she said softly, feeling like there was evidence of their actions showing on her face.

"Didn't you think about the danger of being out there alone?"

"I did, but mainly I didn't want to endanger you or Jackson any longer. I thought if I stayed away, then maybe the bad guys would leave you alone, and those women from church would be satisfied."

In some ways, she wanted to thank the women for coming over and sending her running. Because of them, Jackson had come to find her, and now she realized she'd fallen deeply in love with him.

If they survived until the cavalry arrived, then she would have to leave, so he could have his church. Because no matter what he said, she didn't believe his parishioners would ever accept her as his wife.

"Those women are never happy and can you blame them? They want Jackson to marry their daughters."

He hung his hat on a peg beside the door. "Never happening."

"No, it's not going to happen," Margaret said, scowling at him. "You're going to m—"

"What happened while I was gone?" Hannah asked, interrupting the woman. She didn't want Margaret to say those words. She didn't want anyone to force Jackson into marriage, and she still believed she would be departing as soon as Elliott was caught. She'd leave here broken hearted, deeply in love with a man she could never have.

Margaret shook her head. "You missed a luncheon. Next time those women get together, I may serve them a dose of castor oil just to clean out their systems of all the poison they hang onto."

Hannah smiled and tried to hold back the smirk she could feel lurking on the edges of her mouth. She shook her head as she walked toward the bedroom. "You know, Margaret, I tried to warn you they wouldn't take kindly to me."

"You did, but they're Christian women. I expected better from them."

"Give it time, ladies," Jackson said. "Nothing happens overnight, and forgiveness seems to be the hardest emotion of all for people. They'd rather hold a grudge long past the time they're six feet under, pushing up daisies. We're making progress, but now, we need to capture Elliott and the madam."

"Yes, while you were gone, one of the men came by and said he saw the man riding down Main Street. Elliott has returned."

Chapter Fourteen

Jackson had been careless, and now he suffered for having failed to be more alert.

The men had come into the church, and before he could respond, they had knocked him out.

And here he sat in a room in the bordello, being used as bait to trap Hannah. They knew once she learned Jackson had been taken, she would come for him, and they would then force her back to work in the brothel.

He stared at the man who had hurt Hannah. Since his days in the Civil War, he'd never had the urge to kill another human being. But if Jackson had a gun now, he wouldn't hesitate to kill Elliott. And while Jackson was a godly man and tried not to hate anyone, this man made it next to impossible.

Elliott tightened the rope around Jackson's wrists.

"Don't you think you've hurt her enough, Elliott?"

"Did I ask for your opinion?"

"So, how did you kill her mother?" Jackson knew it was probably stupid, but he couldn't resist poking at the man. He wanted Elliot to feel a smidgeon of the pain Hannah had suffered.

"Am I going to have to gag you?" Elliott stood and walked in front of Jackson. "It's over. You might as well give up fighting. Hannah will come when I send her a note telling her we're going to kill you if she doesn't turn herself in. Then we'll have both of you."

"And you think she's just going to accept working in the brothel again?"

Did this man not know his stepdaughter at all? There was no way Hannah would meekly do Elliot's bidding. He'd already harmed her once. This time, she would fight him with her last breath. And that's what scared Jackson most of all.

"If she wants you to live, she will."

"But I'm not going to stand by and watch her do something she hates. You'll never convince her to work for you again."

Elliott laughed and leaned against a table. "It doesn't matter what you like or want."

"Because you're going to kill us," Jackson finished for him.

Jackson wasn't afraid of dying, but he didn't like the idea of giving up, and he wasn't going to let this man win. He'd go down fighting as long as he could.

"Everyone has to die sooner or later. Hannah is a valuable commodity who can bring in cash if she accepts her position. You're just the bait to keep her in line."

Jackson shook his head, his hands working behind his back, trying to untie the rope that held him prisoner. He had to get loose before Hannah realized he was missing. Jackson had no doubt she would kill Elliott if she thought he'd harmed Jackson.

Twisting his hands behind his back, Jackson worked frantically, pulling at the knots as the rope rubbed his wrists raw. He only needed a few more minutes, and then he would be free to tackle Elliott.

"You're a wanted man, Elliott. The poster is hanging down by the sheriff's office. You're not going to last much longer."

"That's what you think. I have plans. Big plans and neither you nor Hannah are going to mess them up," he said, taking a sip of his whiskey. "Now we wait for the sun to go down. Then I'll send for Hannah."

~

Hannah walked down the middle of Main Street. She

wanted them to know she was coming, fully armed and ready for a fight. She wore both of her six-shooters on her hips and had her petticoat pistol hidden in her skirt. She'd never killed a man before today, but she refused to shirk her duty. She would do whatever it took to save Jackson.

Walking through the swinging doors into the saloon, she thought it was odd the place was almost deserted, only a few people inside.

Mrs. Hutchins walked down the stairs. "Hannah, its lovely to see you. What brings you back to the brothel?"

"Where's Jackson?"

"One of the girls is taking care of him upstairs." She laughed, the sound so evil Hannah wanted to slap the woman. "It just goes to show you all men are the same. They like a pretty girl."

Jackson would never lay with a woman in the brothel. Mrs. Hutchins was lying. She was trying to upset Hannah, so she'd make a mistake.

"I don't believe you. What has Elliott done with him?"

Tim had told her Elliott and the sheriff had taken Jackson. She knew he was in this building somewhere, and she aimed to find him.

"Whatever makes you think Elliott is here?"

Like a queen, Emily strolled the rest of the way down the stairs into the saloon. Memories flooded Hannah, and she bit her lip to keep them at bay. She didn't want to think about what went on upstairs. It was so different from what she'd experienced in Jackson's arms, but she had to find Jackson and rescue him before they killed him.

"Look, I know it's me you want. You bring Jackson out and I'm yours." She was lying. She knew she was lying, but she didn't care. She would never willingly go back to this lifestyle. It had never been a choice, and it wasn't today either.

"Follow me," Mrs. Hutchins said, leading Hannah up the stairs.

When they reached the top, she stopped. "Your guns. I can't allow you to have your weapons any longer."

"Not until I see Jackson. I'm not staying unless you prove to me you have Jackson and you release him."

The woman made a move toward her like she intended to take the guns, and Hannah whipped both six-shooters out, pointing them at the madam. "Take me to Jackson, or I promise you'll be so full of holes you won't float in brine."

The woman scowled, raising her fist. "You're going to regret this." Then she glanced down at the guns and back into Hannah's eyes. For the first time, Hannah thought she saw fear in the woman's gaze.

A calm sense of satisfaction filled Hannah. No matter what happened today, before she left, the madam would wish she'd never brought Hannah into the brothel.

"No," she said defiantly. "No more regrets."

The madam gave her a bewildered look. Never before had Hannah stood up for herself. In the past, she'd tried to run away, but she'd never been impertinent to the woman. This Hannah was stronger, more secure, and no longer afraid.

"Follow me," the madam said, walking down a hall that contained her private quarters. She opened a door and stood to the side. "He's in here."

"You first," Hannah said, pointing her guns toward the madam, indicating she should go in the door.

The woman shrugged and walked inside.

Glancing around, Hannah stepped through the door, but the moment her eyes landed on Jackson's slumped form sitting in a chair, she panicked. The man she'd fallen in love with was being held hostage, and she'd do whatever it took to get him released. "Jackson."

Her stepfather stepped out of the shadows, lunging at her, knocking one of her guns out of her hands. She screamed as he backhanded her across the face, sending her to her knees. He grabbed the other gun from her hand, and she pulled the trigger. The bullet went through the sleeve of his shirt but missed his flesh.

He tried to pry her fingers off the cool metal, causing one to snap. Pain radiated up her hand, and the gun fell to the floor.

"Damn you!" he screamed. "You've caused enough trouble. I should just kill you." He towered over her.

She scooted back and slowly rose from the floor. "What did you do to Jackson?"

"You two seem mighty sweet on each other. Did our little Hannah enjoy her time with the good preacher?"

"Shut up, Elliott." Tears welled in her eyes, and she knew she couldn't let them see her cry, or it would go worse for both of them. But Jackson just sat there, his head hanging like he'd been knocked unconscious.

"I caught him untying his hands and had to show him he's not getting away!" Elliot shouted. "And neither are you. You two have stirred up more trouble than a den of rattlesnakes."

"Fine, I'm here. Now let Jackson go."

Elliott's mouth turned up in a smile that didn't reach his eyes. "You didn't really believe we would let him go, did you?"

Hannah knew she had to get control of this situation. She had to manipulate Elliott. "The Texas Rangers have been spotted right outside of town."

He stared at her a moment. "You're lying."

"No, I'm not. When I shot you, we contacted them. We've been waiting for them to arrive, and they finally showed up. That's also when I learned that not only did you kill my mother, you killed your first wife. You're a murderer, Elliott."

"Your mother was killed because she learned what I was doing for Mrs. Hutchins. She caught me bringing a young woman to the brothel and confronted me. She fell going down the stairs." He shrugged. "Not my fault."

Fury rose inside Hannah like a firestorm in July. She ached with the need to yank up her skirt and pull her pistol out, but she feared it would only waste a good opportunity.

A noise from Jackson had her running to his side. He shook his head, and blood trickled down his face from a cut above his eye.

"Did you have to hit him?"

"He was trying to escape."

"Hannah, don't do this," Jackson said groggily.

"Jackson, the Texas Rangers are not far from town. They'll be here soon."

He grinned and let his head fall to his chest. "I knew they would come."

Unfortunately, Hannah was lying. There'd been no sign of anyone coming. And even if Tim sent a telegram, it would be at least two days before anyone arrived. They could all be dead by then.

Mrs. Hutchins stepped out of the shadows. "I'm going to have one of my men ride out of town and see what he learns."

And now the madam would get confirmation that no one was here. Hannah was running out of time.

"Good idea," Elliott said.

"In the meantime, I think Hannah should get back into her saloon girl clothes. We need her working the floor tonight."

Hannah swallowed, fear racing along her spine. She couldn't do this again. She just couldn't, but Elliot held a gun on her that was larger than her petticoat pistol.

"I'll get her dress," Mrs. Hutchins said, walking from the room. In a moment, she returned and handed the hated outfit to Hannah including the white gloves that she detested. "Get dressed. You're available starting now.."

The madam left the room, and Hannah looked from her stepfather to Jackson.

"Don't do it, Hannah," Jackson said. "Wait, the Rangers will be here soon."

She wished they would bust through the door, but her lie would soon be revealed, and all it had bought her was some extra time. But no matter what, she wasn't going to work in the brothel.

"Strip," Elliott said. "I might want to partake of your pleasures after I see what you've got."

A shiver rippled through her. He'd die at her bare hands before she let him touch her.

Hannah began to unbutton her blouse. She had to get to her petticoat pistol. She stopped. Maybe she could distract him another way. Slowly she pulled on the white gloves.

"You know, Elliott, I've seen the way you look at Mrs. Hutchins. The sheriff is not going to put up with you trying to take his woman." She suspected he wanted Emily Hutchins, and that was why her mother had had the accident.

"What are you talking about?"

"You and Mrs. Hutchins."

"We have a business relationship, nothing more."

Hannah shook her head, hoping to divert him. If she could get him to lower his weapon, then she could pull her gun and shoot him.

Elliott continued to blather on about how his relationship with the madam was nothing more than business.

Hannah interrupted him. "But you want it to be more." She lifted her skirt like she was changing her clothes, knowing she wasn't shedding anything in front of this man.

"That's none of your business."

"True, but the sheriff isn't going to want to share Mrs. Hutchins with anyone. She's all his."

"Why aren't you dressed yet?"

She pulled her pistol out from beneath her petticoats and pointed the gun at him. "Drop your weapon."

He threw back his head and laughed, and Hannah knew it was good for him not to feel threatened by her weapon. "That pistol isn't big enough to do any damage."

"It'll kill a man."

Elliott considered her words then pointed his gun at Jackson. "This one will blow him clear into heaven. And that's what I'm going to do if you don't drop your weapon, now."

Terror gripped her. She couldn't let Elliot hurt Jackson. If she took a shot, Elliot would shoot the man she loved, but if she didn't, Elliot would kill them both.

"Hannah, keep your gun," Jackson cried.

Her hand was shaking. She didn't want to be the reason Jackson died. She didn't want him hurt because of her. And she didn't want Jackson disappointed in her because she'd killed a man. But this was the man she hated. The man who'd killed her mother.

What did she do?

"Drop your gun now, or he's dead," Elliott said, cocking the hammer.

"Shoot him, Hannah," Jackson cried.

For the last six months of her life, she'd dreamed of nothing more than killing this man, and now when the time had come, she wavered. Could she live with herself knowing she'd taken a man's life, even when he deserved to die?

Elliott fired his gun at Jackson.

In horror, she watched Jackson's body fall backwards. The sound of his head hitting the floor and the grunt that escaped his mouth filled her with rage. Screaming, she fired her weapon, the jolt of the small pistol causing her to jump. Her bullet slammed into Elliott's leg.

Shrieking in pain, he fell to the floor, clutching his leg.

Tears streamed down her face as she ran to Elliott and kicked his gun out of reach. Then she picked it up and hit him across the face with it, knocking him out. He was lucky she didn't kill him.

Fearing the worst, she went to Jackson. The man she loved was dead because of her. He lay on the floor, not moving, still tied up in the chair that was now in pieces on the floor. Quickly, she untied his hands and removed the broken chair from his body.

"Jackson," she cried, kneeling down beside his unmoving body, holding his head in her white gloved hands. "I'm so so sorry. I love you. Please don't be dead. Please."

Leaning over him, she tried to find a heartbeat and started to pray. "Oh God, I promise I'll forgive you and attend church every Sunday, if only you'll let him live. Please don't take him from me. Please, God. Please." Sobbing, she lay her head down on his chest, not hearing his heart, knowing he was dead. The man she loved had died because of her.

Suddenly, she felt his hand rubbing her back.

"Jackson?" she said, raising her head and staring into his darkened brown eyes.

"Hannah," he said weakly.

"Where are you hit?" she asked.

"I don't know. It felt like someone knocked the air

from my lungs. Then everything went dark."

Glancing at his clothes, she noticed the bullet hole in this shirt. She stuck her finger through the ragged ends, expecting to feel blood, but all she felt was paper. "What's this?"

He gazed down at his shirt, smiled, and pulled a small Bible from his pocket. Caught in the pages was a bullet. He stared at her, and Hannah could see the shock on his face. "How could that be?"

Taking the book from his hands, she saw how the bullet had gone through the front leather cover, the pages, then lodged itself in the back leather jacket. It had not even broken Jackson's skin.

Shaking her head, she stared in awe at him. "Your Bible protected you. Thank God, it protected you and kept you safe."

His brown eyes filled with tears. "I think God had a reason to let me live."

"You're alive," she sobbed.

"Hannah, I love you," he said, reaching up to caress the side of her face. "I've loved you for weeks."

"Oh, Jackson," she said. "I love you too."

Hearing her stepfather moaning, she sensed they weren't out of danger. "Let's get out of here before the madam returns with her henchmen. Come on, I know a way out."

She yanked off the hated gloves and threw them on the floor. Then she helped him stand.

At first, he was unsteady, but then he took her arm and wrapped it around his waist. "Let's get out of here. The Rangers can take care of Elliott."

Once they were out of the room and heading down the back stairs, Hannah glanced at Jackson. "About the Rangers…I lied."

~

When Jackson and Hannah reached the street, they noticed people running like a herd of cattle were chasing them down the street.

Jackson stopped a man. "What's wrong?"

The man's eyes were wide. "The Texas Rangers just rode into town along with the cavalry from Fort Griffin. If you've got a price on your head, you better get out of town, now."

Jackson laughed, the sound full of happiness and relief. "Thanks, but I'm good."

"Really, I lied," Hannah said.

"I just think you were a bit premature with their arrival," Jackson said, brushing his lips across hers. "This means the town will soon be cleaned up."

An explosion boomed from inside the brothel, sending glass flying out into the street as flames shot up into the air. Jackson covered Hannah with his body, pressing her down as debris fell around them.

People raced with pails of water and started a bucket brigade to keep the fire from spreading to the rest of the town.

"Elliott is in there and the girls," Hannah said. "We have to save the girls!"

"Let's go," Jackson said.

They rushed around the back of the whorehouse, from where they'd just escaped. Girls stood in the windows, crying for help. Hannah ran inside the way she'd come, climbing the stairs with Jackson following. Smoke billowed around them, making it difficult to breathe.

When she reached the hall, all she could see were flames.

"We can't reach them," Jackson said.

Hannah screamed, and several girls heard her, popping their heads out of their bedroom doors. "Come this way!"

Opening a closet, she pulled out blankets.

Fear raged through her; her heart thumped like a wild ride across the prairie. She didn't want to burn here in the brothel, but she couldn't leave without helping the girls escape the blaze.

The women hurried toward her, running through the blaze that now consumed the furniture, their clothes catching on fire. When they reached Hannah and Jackson, they beat back the flames on the women's clothes then showed them the hidden staircase that led outside.

Before Hannah could stop him, Jackson pulled a blanket over his head and ran through the fire.

She screamed. "Stop! No! Jackson, no!"

Paying her no heed, he disappeared into the flames. After what they'd just gone through, why would he risk his life again for her worthless stepfather?

Minutes passed and she felt her heart sink, fearing the worst.

Feeling like it had been hours, when it had only been but a few moments, she waited inside the burning building. Knowing Jackson had gone back for Elliott, she was furious Jackson would risk his life for that piece of dung. The smoke almost overpowered her, but she refused to leave.

Suddenly, through the flames, she saw Jackson emerge with two more women and Elliott.

The preacher man had saved her hated stepfather. Yes, she wanted to see him hang, but not at the expense of the man she loved.

Limping, they hurried through the inferno. She waited with blankets. When they came through the flames, she beat their clothing until they no longer smoldered.

Standing in the hallway, they heard the ominous sound of cracking.

Glancing up, she saw the roof above them was about to collapse, the noise sending shudders through her.

"Everyone down the stairs!" Jackson screamed over the roar of the fire.

Hannah grabbed the other side of her stepfather, and together, they practically dragged him down the stairs. She didn't understand why Jackson hadn't just let the man die. She didn't understand why he couldn't have left him to burn, but then she realized this was Jackson.

He would never step back and let someone suffer, even if he were deserving of his fate. He was still God's child, and she either had to accept that about the man or move on.

When they reached the streets, a Texas Ranger rode up. Jackson handed Elliott to the lawman. "Elliott Potter, wanted for the murder of Georgia Potter and suspected of killing Mary Williams Potter. Plus, there are two warrants out on him for kidnapping and selling women into prostitution."

The lawman took Elliott and tied his hands behind his back. "You're hereby taken into custody."

"What about Mrs. Hutchins? Did she get out of the saloon?" Hannah asked the lawman, curious to know what had become of the hated woman.

"No, ma'am. She was shot by the sheriff who then started the fire in the saloon to cover her murder."

"What? How do you know? Who turned in the sheriff?" Hannah asked.

Tim from the stables stepped up. "I did, Hannah. I saw him shoot Mrs. Hutchins to keep her from leaving town when they learned the Rangers had arrived. They've already arrested him."

"Oh, my God, Tim. If I hadn't asked for your help, he

might have gotten away with her murder," Hannah said, hugging the young man's neck. "Thank you. Thank you for helping us."

He nodded. "I was in the saloon, trying to find you, when I heard the argument. I was going to help her, when he shot her." He shrugged nonchalantly. "I hid until I saw him setting the gunpowder on fire. Then I hightailed it out of there."

"Thanks, Tim," Hannah repeated.

Elliott sighed. "We could have made so much money together."

The Texas Ranger shook his head. "Let's get you to jail. Then I'll have the doctor tend to your leg."

Jackson and Hannah watched the Texas Ranger haul off Elliott with Tim following. As they disappeared into the jail, Hannah turned to Jackson.

"It's over," she said with a sigh. "We did it. We cleaned up the town."

"Yes, so now you have no excuse not to marry me."

Her chest ached, and she wanted with all her being to say yes, but she just knew it wouldn't be right. It wouldn't be fair to Jackson. He deserved a wife who would be accepted by everyone. "Your church is never going to welcome me. You're better off without me."

"Well, I have an idea on how you can change how they refer to you. How does Mrs. Jackson Colster, Sheriff of Hide Town, Texas, sound?"

"What? Are you crazy?" *Sheriff?*

She could continue the job of cleaning up this town. She would refuse to let anyone who was wanted by the law to reside here, and she'd make certain the saloon, if rebuilt, was run properly. But no, she couldn't stay here because of Jackson.

"Listen to me. You could use your bounty hunting skills, but instead of traveling around the country catching criminals, you would be doing it right here in our town. And you could also do your duties as a preacher's wife, at least until we had kids, and then you might be kind of busy taking care of them."

This was why she couldn't stay. He deserved to be happy, and she couldn't be around when he finally married another woman. Watching him with someone else would break her heart. She had to leave.

"Jackson, I love you with all my heart and soul, but I refuse to become your wife and have your church not accept me. It wouldn't be fair to you or me."

"Our love should not be about my church. It should be about the two of us. If they refuse to see how wonderful you are, then we find a new congregation. It's simple."

"But your church is a part of who you are. No one is going to accept an ex-soiled dove."

His brows drew together, and his eyes flashed with anger. "Okay, I agree with you my church is a part of who I am, but you said a very important word. *Ex*-soiled dove. We all have pasts. We all have sin. It's time you put the past behind you and started fresh."

"I agree, and I want to start fresh." She really did, but she loved him way too much to let her past hurt him.

Jackson took a deep breath, gazed into her eyes. "I don't want to live without you. You're more important to me than any congregation. And they're going to love you like I do, once they know you." He picked up her hands. "Will you marry me?"

Hannah thought about it for a moment. It was what she wanted. She loved this man. She wanted to have his babies, to grow old together, and to love him each night. But could his church find it in their hearts to love her as she was?

"I would love to be your wife if your church will accept me."

He leaned over and kissed her on the mouth, right in the middle of Main Street. "I love you, Hannah Williams. You better find yourself a wedding dress because there is soon going to be a wedding."

Chapter Fifteen

The next Sunday, Margaret and Hannah sat in the front pew of the church. When they had come through the door, people had stopped and greeted her, saying hello and how good it was to see her. They acted like she was their long-lost best friend, and several times she'd been shocked at how nice they were. She'd received two invitations to lunch and one to tea.

"Margaret, what did you promise them or should I say threaten them with?" she asked.

"Not a thing," Margaret said. "Though I did read some scriptures to several ladies."

After the Song-leader sang a few songs and a man came up and led the prayer, Jackson took the podium.

At first Hannah felt fearful of what he would say, but then he held everyone's attention.

"Good morning! I can't tell you how glad I am to be with you today." He held up his Bible, the one he carried in his pocket—the one that still had the bullet meant to kill him stuck in the leather cover.

The crowd gasped.

"I shouldn't be here this morning. I should be dead. I was going to give a sermon on forgiveness today. I had it all written out, thought it was a fine lesson. Then yesterday, when the shooting started and I thought I wouldn't be here today, it came to me. Love is what I should be talking about."

He walked across the built-up platform. "If you read your Bible, you know we are all supposed to love one another. We may not agree with each other's actions, but we're to love and accept each other and let God judge us for our actions here on earth. Not man."

Hannah watched the man she loved with all her heart and knew there was no way she could leave him. Even if his church didn't accept her, he was her heart and soul, and she could no more go off and leave him than not take her next breath.

Yes, he was a preacher, and she was an ex-soiled dove, but he could help her learn to trust God again, and she could help him get over the Civil War and the killing he'd seen. Together, they would help rebuild Hide Town into a community where they could raise their children.

"I want you to know I've fallen in love with Hannah Williams. Yes, I know her past, but did you know I had a past as well? I ran from the Civil War. Sure, I was only ten years old, but I'd seen enough men's bodies torn by bullets and bayonets that I couldn't deal with the carnage. So I ran. I lied and told everyone the general sent me home when I ran because I didn't want to watch another person die.

"Hannah and I are both imperfect human beings that life has tossed about like two souls lost at sea. And now we're joining forces. I hope you will love and accept her the same as me. But if not, we will be moving to another town and a new congregation. We're all imperfect human beings, and we all need God's love."

He stepped down from the podium and came over to where she was sitting. "Hannah, marriage was created by God for two people to join together for a lifetime. I love you." He got down on bended knee. "Will you please marry me and let me show you love for the rest of our lives together?"

Tears welled up in her eyes, and she heard Margaret beside her blubbering like a baby.

She took his hand and pulled him to his feet and stood with him. A tear rolled down her cheek. "Yes, Jackson, I would be honored to be your wife. I love you with all my heart."

He smiled, kissed her on the lips in front of his congregation, then hurried back to the podium.

Love filled every corner of her heart, and she had to wipe the tears of happiness away. For better or worse, she'd just agreed to marry Jackson, and she would spend her days loving him for being a wonderful man.

"Song-leader, please lead us in a song and one more prayer."

Jackson came back down and pulled Hannah to her feet, leading her out the door. Together, they greeted the members of the church as they left the building. Hannah was treated like a treasured member in the congregation, the people in his church opening their arms to her.

After everyone left, Jackson wrapped his arms around her. "So what are we going to do for excitement next week, Miss Williams?"

She laughed. "We're going to get married."

"Oh, I like the way you think."

"Well, do you want to wait?"

"We could do it right this moment as far as I'm concerned."

She thought for a moment. "No, I think we need to let your congregation help with the arrangements."

He smiled, and Hannah felt like his smile touched the center of her heart.

He kissed the tip of her nose. "You mean *our* congregation."

"Oh dear, I'm going to be a preacher's wife."

"And sheriff."

"I feel like I'm letting Ruby down. Who is going to go bounty hunting with her? I guess there's always Caroline."

"Ruby will be just fine. And so will you."

"I love you, Jackson."

"I love you more, Hannah."

His lips covered hers, and she knew she still had healing that would need to happen, but things for now were good, all because she'd been so determined.

~

Zenith, Texas

Caroline Mackenzie sat at the dinner table and listened to her mother and Levy Johnson, pig farmer extraordinaire, talk about what made a great ham. She picked at her food, knowing her mother would expect her to walk him out the door later and let him kiss her goodnight.

She shuddered at the very idea, and he glanced at her concerned. "Are you cold, Miss Caroline? I'd be happy to bring you your shawl."

"No, no, thank you. I'm fine. Just felt like something crawled up my spine there for a moment."

Years of living with a smelly man and bearing his children had flashed before her eyes. She wanted to marry a man for love, not desperation.

Her mother frowned, obviously not happy that Caroline was not participating in the ham discussion. This was the chosen son-in-law, and Caroline was resisting her mother's choice with all her being.

"While I clean up the dishes, why don't you two take a stroll in the yard?" her mother said, beginning to gather the plates from the table.

"Great idea," Levy said. "I brought my harmonica, if you'd like to hear me play."

Joy of joys. Did he think that was going to help her overlook his dirty fingernails and smelly clothes? And good grief, did her mother not see he'd tracked mud on her rugs? Caroline would bet her next trip into town his house was nothing more than one big ole pig sty.

"You know, maybe I *am* coming down with something. I'm starting to feel a mite poorly. If you don't mind, Levy, could we postpone our walk for another time?"

His face fell. She didn't dare look at her mother's face, knowing it would be filled with rage.

"Of course, Caroline." Levy stood and glanced about uneasily. "I'll be heading home. Maybe we can do this again soon."

Her mother walked to him. "Levy, I'll invite you over again next week. Maybe we could play some cards after dinner. Let you and Caroline spend some time getting to know each other."

He glanced at Caroline. She gave him her best, *don't even bother* smiles. She didn't want to marry this man.

As soon as he was out the door, her mother turned on her. "I don't know what you think you're doing, missy, but he's about your last chance at marriage."

Caroline flipped her long black hair away from her shoulders. "I'm barely twenty. That's not ancient."

"Caroline, I'm serious. You need to marry that man. He's good, he's decent, and I'm not going to be around to support you for many more years. It's time you found a husband. I'm going to talk to him next week, and we will announce your engagement soon afterwards."

Taking a deep breath, Caroline stared at her mother, anger rushing through her like a flash flood. "Momma, you're not making this decision for me. I'll find my own husband, and it won't be Levy Johnson."

Her mother faced her, her hands on her hips. "I've given you plenty of time, and you're not even interested in looking at a man. Next week, you're engaged."

"That's not true. I've been looking."

"No, you've been spending time with Ruby, learning how to shoot, instead of learning how to be a good wife."

"I just want to be able to take care of myself."

"Well, I've done the looking for you, and Levy Johnson is a fine man. And he would love for you to be his wife."

Caroline shook her head, stunned at how far her mother had gone behind her back to find her a husband. "No, Mother. I'm not marrying him."

Her mother took a deep breath. "Then you have until next week to find me someone better."

Turning on her heel, Caroline walked to her bedroom. No, she wouldn't be here next week to announce her engagement. She wouldn't be here in the morning.

The time had come for her to go out on her own. Ruby had trained her—she knew how to shoot, she knew how to ride, she knew how to scout for criminals. Now it was her turn to go hunting as a bounty hunter.

Thank You For Reading!

Dear Reader,

Sometimes a story just flows from my fingertips out onto the pages and sometimes I wonder why I wanted to write about these characters! While I thoroughly loved these two people, I struggled with balancing the amount of religion to show in the story. Putting a preacher with a soiled dove was difficult while trying to show his faith and heal her enough that she could become a preacher's wife. Jackson developed into one of my favorite characters simply because I loved how he overcame a terrible childhood. Hannah has always been a tough character to write as I can't imagine being sold into that lifestyle. Together they stretched me as a writer and I hope you enjoyed their story.

I have one small request. If you're inclined, please leave a review. Whether or not you loved the book or hated, it-I'd enjoy your feedback. Reviews are difficult to obtain and have the power to make or break a book.

Reading one of my books is like spending time with me, and I just want to say Thank You from the bottom of my heart.

Yours in Drama, Divas, Bad Boys and Romance!
Sincerely,
Sylvia McDaniel

Books by Sylvia McDaniel

Contemporary Romance

Standalones
The Reluctant Santa
My Sister's Boyfriend
The Wanted Bride
The Relationship Coach
Her Christmas Lie
Secrets, Lies, and Online Dating
Paying for the Past
Cupid's Revenge

Anthologies
Kisses, Laughter & Love
Christmas with you

Collaborative Series

Magic, New Mexico
Touch of Decadence

Western Historicals

Standalones
A Hero's Heart
A Scarlet Bride
Second Chance Cowboy

The Cuvier Women
Wronged
Betrayed
Beguiled

Lipstick and Lead
Desperate
Deadly
Dangerous
Daring
Determined
Deceived

Scandalous Suffragettes
Abigail
Bella
Callie
Faith

The Burnett Brides
The Rancher Takes a Bride
The Outlaw Takes a Bride
The Marshal Takes a Bride
The Christmas Bride

Anthologies
Wild Western Women
Courting the West
Wild Western Women Ride Again

Collaborative Series

The Surprise Brides
Ethan

American Mail Order Brides
Katie

About the Author

Sylvia McDaniel is a best-selling, award-winning author of historical romance and contemporary romance novels. Known for her sweet, funny, family-oriented romances, Sylvia is the author of The Burnett Brides, a western historical western series, The Cuvier Widows, a Louisiana historical series, and several short contemporary romances.

She is the former President of the Dallas Area Romance Authors, a member of the Romance Writers of America®, and a member of Novelists Inc. Her novel, A Hero's Heart, was a 1996 Golden Heart Finalist. Several other books have placed or won in the San Antonio Romance Authors Contest and the LERA Contest, and she was a Golden Network Finalist.

Married for nearly twenty years to her best friend, they

have two dachshunds that are beyond spoiled and a good-looking, grown son who thinks there's no place like home. She loves gardening, shopping, knitting, and football (Cowboys and Bronco's fan), but not necessarily in that order.

Look for her the first Tuesday of every month at the Plotting Princesses blogspot, and be sure to sign up for her newsletter to learn about new releases and contests. Every month a new subscriber is entered into a drawing for a free book!

She can be found online at: www.sylviamcdaniel.com or on Facebook. You can write to Sylvia at P.O. Box 2542, Coppell, TX 75019.